Angels of Hells Canyon

by

Kevin Royce White

Cover Photo courtesy of Ron Cuoio/Idaho Photography copyright 2010.

ISBN: 1481239937
ISBN 13: 9781481239936
Library of Congress Control Number: 2012923690
CreateSpace Independent Publishing Platform
North Charleston, South Carolina

Dedication

To my friends whose personalities brought the characters of my story to life, you are all very special to me. To Ms. Paula Silici, my mentor, who challenged me to pursue my dream and guided me down this path. To Mr. Ron Cuoio who gifted me with the use of his art, a stranger who had paused momentarily to take a photo, ironically at the same location where I had stood fifteen years before. Through his lens, Ron's photographic skill truly captured the magnificent grandeur of the peaks of the Seven Devils of Hells Canyon, Idaho.

To all who have worked so hard to preserve and protect the Hells Canyon recreation area, I salute you. To the wonderful residents of northern Idaho whose welcoming character and love of nature allowed me to build the backdrop for my story, I thank you. To the people of the Nez Perce Indian Nation whose history, sufferings, legends and cultural roots added the special patina to my story, I graciously thank and am proud to acknowledge.

Most of all, I dedicate this story to my best friend, my wife Darlene. Through her love and dedication, I was provided with the foundation, that only she could give, which allowed me to weave Dan's love for Hanna and Maggie into the fabric of my story; she is without a doubt, my *Guardian Angel.*

Prologue

We live on a planet with a billion other souls. Though we are all of different minds, we do share one thing in common: dreams of places or things that most of us will never see or possess. For those who believe that special things do happen, the miracle of life unfolds effortlessly in front of our eyes. For the magic of life to truly be realized, we only have to open our hearts and believe that all things are possible.

Some among us pass through our lives who have chosen to rise above their own self- interests, to give to others more than they take, to dedicate themselves, not for their own rewards, accolades, or fame, but to promote the happiness and safety of others. These are God's creatures who have been crowned for all eternity with the mystical title of "Guardian Angel."

Do Angels exist? If so, what makes them do the things they do? Has Almighty God provided them for us so they may step in and do His bidding when all else has gone awry? Or do they just exist in our minds to give us hope in times of desperation?

Are they the spirits mentioned in times past, those heavenly beings chosen to remain behind to watch over us and protect all the good in us?

Are they gladiators fighting against fate for those who have found themselves in a truly untenable situation where now only an angel can change their destiny?

There are ordinary places on this planet that we all call home, but there are also places we sometimes chance to visit that are so magnificent they could have only been created by the Almighty Himself for a special purpose. In my travels west from the Rocky Mountains to visit my old friend David Freeman, I came upon such a place.

I stopped my car on the side of the road at a place called Windy Gap. Leaving the vehicle, I walked slowly down a narrow path of powdery ancient volcanic dust, leaving my footprints where thousands of others had traveled before me. I was about to encounter a place given the ominous name Hells Canyon. Slowly, one after another, rising majestically from the valley floor, I saw them. Like the mighty arms of God reaching up from the canyon floor, the peaks of the Seven Devils stretched toward the sky.

These magical monoliths filled the valley between Oregon and Idaho with great beauty and ferocity. My heart began to race as I neared the edge of the precipice overlooking North America's deepest canyon, a mighty gorge more than 6,000 feet below me. The scene that filled my eyes could have only been painted by the hand of God Himself.

God had created before me, a vast canvas. He had danced a brush laden with all the colors of the rainbow, blending and shading each hue into a masterpiece unrivaled by any mortal man.

This was not a place set aside for the Devil or his minions; this was a magnificent wonderland springing forth from the Creator for only one thing. This was a special place created for his Angels to find rest; this was his Angels' Playground.

I backed off a bit, and sat among the wildflowers in a small meadow, trying to soak up every drop of this magical place. With a name like Hells Canyon and mountain peaks named Seven Devils, I had expected to find a lifeless moonscape stretching out before me. These names were more suited for a barren place, a wasteland devoid of all life, a place where God had slashed a nightmarish gash in the earth, its boundaries reaching out like tentacles, thirsting for rain in a mid-July heat wave. What should have lain before me would have been a valley where no man dared to tread, a place representing Hell on Earth set aside for Lucifer to ply his evil trade. But this was not so.

Settling back, I began to calm my heart rate and soak up what I thought was to be the totality of all the grandeur that lay before me. Then, suddenly, a movement in the sky, a blur at first, sharpened in the periphery of my vision.

First one, then two, then dozens of eagles seemed to magically appear all around me. From high in the sky and from the shadows of the tree line they came. Like playful nymphs, they danced across the sky with their white feathered heads glistening in the rays of the sun.

Their massive wings reached out in regal abundance, feathers spreading wide, searching delicately for just the right notes for their symphony to accompany their evening frolic.

From deep in the canyon the breeze increased. It was as if our Creator pursed His lips and began to blow through the treetops of the massive pine forest. I felt as though He was watching with me, providing a current of air as His feathery angels did pirouettes on their dance floor of thermals, flowing up to the heavens on His warm breath.

They were eagles so swift in flight and so many in numbers, I dared not try to count them. To number just one, or to waste one moment of the totality of this dance would have surely been a mistake for which I never could have forgiven myself.

Suddenly, as magically as they had appeared, they vanished. The last of these feathered giants turned his head as if to make his parting bow and bidding farewell. His keen, sparkling eye met mine as he looked into my marveling gaze. Stretching wide his golden beak, he let out a scream that only an eagle can sound. I thought I saw a smile after he caught my gaze of wonder, transfixed as I was on his majestic brilliance.

Slowly, but with great regret for their departure, I rose to my feet. Daylight was fading and I had a hazardous seventeen-mile drive back down the mountain to Riggins where my friend David lived. Tomorrow, yes, maybe tomorrow, David would be able to join me at the top of the mountain. If just one more time these angels of Hells Canyon who had invited me to witness their ballet of wonder would dance once again! David was a good man; maybe they would dance for the both of us.

Chapter 1

As I descended the curves of Hells Canyon Road, the sky had quickly given way to the shades of dusk. A mystical silence surrounded me as ghostly images began to form silhouettes against the darkening forest backdrop, now illuminated only by the glow of my headlights.

To my right, a large bull elk appeared, raised his massive, antlered head, and bugled toward the treetops, announcing his dominant presence to all. Planting his massive hoofs firmly into the embankment, not twenty feet from the roadway, he bowed his massive headdress of sharpened bone, his golden cape emblazoned in the fading light.

Though I did not sense his posture was intended to frighten, it left little doubt that he was firmly advising me that he was a forest elder. Should any outsider dare to harm this magical place, he would not hesitate to defend the sanctity of its Creator with his life.

A sharp turn to the left and the road abruptly narrowed. Slowing to a crawl, I could hear the sound of loosened stones beneath my right tires tumbling off the unguarded shoulder and beyond the sheer drop-off into the blackness of the canyon below.

Forlorn yelps of coyotes invaded the silence from the ridgeline above me as the animals stalked their first victim of the night.

With all of Hells Canyon's beauty, grandeur, and abundance of life, these sounds of hungry predators predicated the clear affirmation that with life comes death. Somewhere in this wilderness tonight, one doe would see her fawn grow to adulthood, while another would mourn within the circle of life.

Cautiously, I made my way down the remaining switchbacks, not wanting to further trespass into the lives of the wildlife that surrounded me. The last thing I needed was to careen off a cliff before I could share the gift that had been given to me this day.

Turning north on Highway 95, the town of Riggins lie just ahead. I had called my friend David the week before to let him know of my arrival. It had been more than fifteen years since I had last seen him and his wife Kris.

It was after 7:00 p.m. when I pulled into the parking lot under the flashing neon sign that announced the Salmon River Motel. Without delay, I checked into a room that featured a small deck overlooking the Salmon River and decided to settle my nerves from the ride out of the canyon with a few ice-cold beers.

I could hear the low roar of the rapids just downstream as I opened the window to take in the night air. As I stepped onto the overhanging deck, the only thing visible was a wide, black ribbon of swirling water. Other than its ominous current, the river posed no threat as it passed, only occasionally pausing to spit up a small geyser of spray as it danced around a pile of submerged ancient boulders. Turning in, I fell asleep to the sound of the rushing water.

Awakened by an ear-splitting Country-Western song blaring from the clock radio that a former guest must have set previous to my arrival, I was welcomed abruptly to the town of Riggins. It was 5:00 am.

I made my way down the street to the River Rock Café, which had been recommended by the motel clerk as one of the best eateries in town. Sitting at the counter, I ordered one of their specialties: corned beef hash, three eggs, and home-cooked potatoes.

Finishing up my gourmet's delight, I looked up just as an Idaho County Sheriff Deputy took a seat in a back booth. He appeared friendly as he nodded and smiled to the other patrons around him. Riggins was such a small town, surely he knew David Freeman. Anyone who had met David, for one reason or another, never forgot him.

Without hesitation, I approached. "Morning Sheriff. Mind if I sit down?"

"Not at all, sir. I'm Deputy Boyd. My boss Sheriff Mears is the guy who makes the real money," he responded with a wide smile.

"It's very nice to meet you Deputy; my name is Kevin White.

After the exchange of a few more pleasantries, I explained that I was looking for a friend but wasn't sure where he lived. David had moved since I had been to Riggins fifteen years before. David had told me that he had a cabin just south of town, but he hadn't been very specific as to its exact location.

"And what would your friend's name be, sir? I know most of the locals in the area. For good or bad, I've made the acquaintance of just about all of them– if they've been here for any length of time."

"His name is Freeman, David Freeman."

Before I could get out another word, Deputy Boyd sat straight up in the booth, folded his arms across his chest in a defensive posture, and focused his eyes on me over the top of his wire-rimmed glasses as if he were about to conduct an interrogation of a suspect. No longer smiling, he slowly tilted his head to one side, sizing me up. He then slowly and deliberately began to speak.

"You say this David Freeman is a friend of yours? He must not be too close of a friend if you're asking strangers like me where he lives. I think you need to be a little more specific regarding your business here in town. Where did you say you were from again?"

I quickly answered his initial questions, and after a few more minutes of verbal dueling, I provided the answers that only a friend of David's would have known. Deputy Boyd's posture once again began to relax. Placing his callused index finger to his lips, he stopped me before I continued speaking.

"As I said before, Riggins is a small town where everyone knows just about everybody. Why don't we make room for some hungry people and go down the street to my office? It's a lot more comfortable and we'll have fewer curious ears to have to deal with, if you know what I mean." Once again he flashed me the same wide smile he had welcomed me with earlier.

"Have a seat, my friend," he said after we entered his office. "So you say you and David are old friends from Oklahoma? Well, I have to say, David's never spoken of you by name, but he did say many times he was from Oklahoma City and that he had done concrete work there. You know, David is a real worker bee, most of the time he works out of town. Not much construction around here. He told me the other day he's working up in the town of White Bird this week, building cabinets for some retired guy. He said if he got finished up, he should be back in town sometime late tonight.

"David's wife Kris won't be home now, either. She works for a television station, and she doesn't get home until after dark most evenings. Now you can see why I don't give out much information to strangers about locals. It keeps the bad guys guessing so they never quite know when someone is going to be on the other side of a door pointing a loaded gun. It kind of helps keep the crime rate down."

Boyd then offered me a ride around town on a quick patrol. We headed south out of town along the Little Salmon River branch to a place called Rapid River where Fish and Game had a hatchery for Chinook salmon.

Boyd suggested that being a "flatlander" and all, I might enjoy a walk down along the river to the hatchery where I could possibly catch a glimpse of the large adult Chinooks making their way back from the Pacific Ocean to the hatchery where they were born.

Returning to his office, he gathered up a fishing rod and a small tackle box for me, and equipping me with a temporary fishing license–which was no more than his business card with a note stating that I was a friend of his–he shuffled me out the door.

"Tell you what. You go catch us some trout for lunch while I do some paperwork, and when you get back I'll give you a tour around town and take you out to where David's place is. Oh, by the way, as far as those big Chinooks go, they're just for the Indians this time of year. That fishing permit in your pocket I gave you won't save you if the game warden catches you with one of them big beauties."

Thinking that Boyd just might be testing my character and honesty, although I was appreciative of the gesture of the business card, I stopped by the general store on the way to Rapid River and purchased a three day, out-of-state fishing license.

Walking along Rapid River, I caught and released more trout in an hour than I had caught in my whole life. Casting from the tops of the ancient boulders into these pristine waters was truly an opportunity of a lifetime. This gift Deputy Boyd had given me, allowing me to cast my eyes upon his personal fishing spot, was one I could surely never repay.

The peace and serenity brought back fond memories of the times when I was a boy fishing with my father on the streams in the Sierra Nevada Mountains of California. Finding myself now baiting a line along this world-class trout stream was far more than I had ever expected.

My trip to Windy Gap the previous day and what I was experiencing now, left no doubt that I had not only found my way to God's Art Studio and the Playground for Angels, I had been granted the privilege of becoming a character in one of God's personal paintings.

Keeping six of the larger trout, toward noon I headed back into town. It was time I refocus on my objective of reuniting with my friend.

"Well, my oh my," Boyd said as I strode into his office and held up my catch. "From the looks of that stringer, even an old Okie flatlander can get lucky here in Idaho," Boyd said, giggling like a kid who had just shared his secret fishing spot with a new friend.

"I sort of took the rest of the day off to show you around the area if you like, but if I'm imposing just let me know. If anyone asks who you are, I'll just tell them that you're a prisoner. That'll give them something to gossip about."

After a short tour of the town, we headed south on Highway 95 to a dirt road just south of town.

"Here it is, FSRD 1614. The FSRD stands for Forest Service Road, but we call it Big Salmon Road. It runs way back up into the canyon along the river. Just up ahead you'll see a barn and some mules in a corral. If the sign is up and some shithead hasn't shot the damn thing off the post again, we'll make a right at the sign that says FS254. David's place is just past the barn about a tenth of a mile." Turning just where he had said, we wandered into the woods on a dirt road–for what Boyd had estimated to be about two miles–where the road made a switchback at a sign that read Dead End.

Leave it to David to find the most remote place possible to build a cabin. I had always known that David was somewhat of a loner, but this place was so deep in the woods that he had better really love himself, and Kris had better really love him, too.

"That's David's place there to the left, and that last structure about a hundred yards farther down is the old Rawlins place. David pretty much looks over it for their daughter Maggie. She doesn't come around here much anymore."

Knowing that David and Kris weren't home, I suggested we return to town. I didn't want to take uninvited liberties by walking around the property.

"Sheriff...."

"Let's drop the Sheriff, okay? I would prefer you call me Dennis. You obviously know now that David is my friend as well, and any friend of David's is certainly a friend of mine."

"Well, Dennis, if you'll take me back into town, I'd like to clean up, and it would be my honor if you and your wife would join me tonight for dinner. The man at the motel said they serve a pretty nice steak at that River Rock Café."

"Thanks for your gracious offer, but I have to decline. My wife already advised me that we have plans this evening with the relatives. If the offer still stands, maybe we can all get together some evening before you leave for home. I'm sure my wife Ruby would enjoy it as well."

"Done and done!" I quickly agreed.

It was just after dark when I'd finished dinner and made a phone call to David. I told him that I had arrived in town the night before and was excited to come out to his place that evening for a visit. It was about an hour later when I approached the dead end. I found him standing in the middle of the road, dressed in faded jeans and a Pendleton shirt.

"David, my friend, it's been a long time. You haven't changed a bit. A little greyer up top, maybe, same scraggly beard, but other than that I'd know you anywhere. Give me a hug you old grouchy bastard. Where's Kris? Is she here?"

With a slow wave of his callused hand across his chest, and with a shallow bow, he turned toward his cabin. "Ask and you shall receive!"

Standing in the doorway, outlined by the warm glow of a coal oil lamp stood Kris. She looked just as pretty and reserved as she always had. Dressed in an ankle-length 1800s-period dress, I knew that she had made a special effort to dress up for my arrival.

"Kris Freeman, you look just as beautiful as ever, girl. I still can't figure out what in the hell you ever saw in this grungy old man of yours!"

"You look good, too, old man! Now you two get on in here," she added with a playful giggle.

The interior of the cabin was just what I had expected it would be. The home the two of them had built together was simply spectacular in every detail, one that would have been prized by any early explorer stumbling upon this forested hideaway.

Built of native logs that had been hewed by hand, David's skills as a carpenter were definitely apparent. Not only the structure, but the furniture within–including tables, chairs, and a chandelier supporting five small coal oil lamps in the center of the main room– had obviously been lovingly crafted by my friend's now weathered hands.

Had it not been for the few modern conveniences in the kitchen area and the indoor plumbing, one could have easily thought they'd been transported back in time to a cabin built by Daniel Boone himself.

In the bathroom off the main room, the theme continued. To the left of a claw-foot bathtub, a waterproofed curtain of tan-colored canvas was held open by a tanned strap of animal hide. The ingenious curtain framed a shower stall that featured a polished copper pipe and a hammered copper shower head that protruded from the redwood wall planking above the hand-soldered floor pan. On the opposing wall David had mounted a redwood water closet atop a polished copper pole with a pull chain adorned with a scarlet red tassel.

From the hand-forged metal sink bowl and flat iron door hinges, to the frosted glass in the transom above the plank door, the two of them had truly created a first-class, "throne room" befitting any western-style abode.

The interior walls of the main room had been adorned with tanned hides from the local critters that had fallen to David's keen hunting skills, including a magnificent black bearskin rug prominently displayed in the center of the floor.

Kris, too, had added her loving touch. Perfectly placed handmade crocheted doilies on the table tops supported wood-framed sepia photos of her and David, as well as those taken of their other special friends and relatives.

"You two have certainly outdone yourselves. Your home is just beautiful! Now, tell me what you guys have been up to for all these years."

"I have to say right off the bat, Kris and I were just thrilled when Dennis called us this morning and told us that you were in town. He said that he had driven you out here this morning."

So much for my thinking that Dennis Boyd had relied on his cop's senses in determining that I was a good guy and all. While I had been out fishing, Boyd had contacted David on the phone and verified my "old friend" story before he ever would have considered showing me where David lived.

Kris prepared supper while David and I reminisced about old times and brought each other up to date on things that had transpired over the past several years. While most of the time Kris sat quietly listening to my stories of Oklahoma, she commented more than once on how disappointed she was that my wife Darlene hadn't joined me on the trip.

After finally convincing her that my original plans had been to travel to Colorado to do some fishing and that this detour had simply been a last minute decision, she forgave me for Darlene's absence.

It was almost midnight when I finally told them that I had to return to my motel. Although they were more than willing to extend their utmost hospitality by fixing me a place to sleep, they agreed to let me leave, only on the promise that I gather up my stuff and return the next morning with my things. They wouldn't hear anything more about my staying at a motel in town. Their home was my home, and that was that!

Had it not been for the exhausting day the day before, the 5 a.m. sounds around the motel probably wouldn't have gone unnoticed, but it was almost seven before I arose, showered, gathered my things, and headed for the office to checkout.

"Morning, sir. It looks like you'll be leaving us," the desk clerk said, flashing me a broad smile. "Everything has already been taken care of. Deputy Boyd stopped by last evening and said you'd probably be checking out. There will be no charge for your stay. I hope you have a wonderful time for the rest of your trip."

Puzzled, I thanked him for his hospitality and generosity, although I didn't quite understand it. As I walked to my car I wondered just what else my new friend Deputy Boyd had taken care of for me without my knowledge. After picking up some groceries to lessen any burden on David and Kris during my stay, I headed back to their cabin.

It was just about nine when I pulled up in David's lane. He was outside speaking to a man standing next to a large mule in the corral.

"Well, it's about time you got your ass out of bed," David quipped.

"Everything go okay at the motel?" the second man chimed in.

It was Deputy Boyd, this time not in uniform but dressed like a cowhand preparing to go on a cattle drive. After a short exchange of pleasantries, I thanked Boyd for his benevolence in taking care of my bill, and the three of us headed inside.

The cabin was filled with the aroma and the sizzling sounds of bacon frying. "Have a seat, old man," Kris said, smiling. "You're obviously not used to these country schedules, I see. David's been up since five waiting for you and his breakfast. If you had taken any longer to get here, I believe he would have eaten one of his boots."

While we had breakfast, Dennis informed us that although it was his day off, he had gotten information about some men who had been putting in a Marijuana grow up in one of the canyons a few miles east of David's place. He had stopped by to borrow David's mule Molly, and ride up to the canyon to investigate and verify the information before taking further action.

David had offered to go along for support, but Dennis declined his offer. This would just be a trip to reconnoiter the situation, not to be making any arrests. He would make this trip alone, not wanting to arouse any suspicion or to put David in any danger should the information be accurate.

As I watched his departure down a trail that disappeared into the surrounding forest, I thought to myself how many times this scene had replicated itself back in the old days:

A lawman mounted on his horse heading out alone into the unknown to uphold the law.

"Well, now. Kris has to go down to Boise for a few days, and since that just leaves the two of us, how about we take a walk around and I can show you the place?" David said

Bidding goodbye to Kris, I assured her that I would be here when she returned. David, who had stepped inside while I talked to Kris, reemerged from the cabin and waved, looking just like he had stepped out of a set of a John Wayne western. On his head he sported a wide-rimmed brown Stetson adorned with the skin of a timber rattlesnake, with two inches of what remained of its broken rattles resting on the sweat-stained brim. Around his waist hung a gun belt on which was holstered a Colt Peacemaker poised for action in one of the most beautiful hand-engraved leather holsters I had ever seen.

"Just where in the hell are you taking me, anyway?"

"You asked about the old Rawlins cabin, didn't you? Well, come on. Let's go and check it out. You can take a peek at what a real settler's place used to look like."

Traversing east to what was once a well-worn pathway now overgrown with fern boughs emerging from the encroaching forest floor, we came upon a meadow illuminated by the morning sun.

There it stood like a ghostly form, silent and alone, a cobwebbed settler's cabin frozen in time. It was as if those who had once filled those log walls with love, laughter, and joy had simply walked away.

Stacked firewood slumped next to the front porch rotting and unused. Through the dusty window panes, the lace curtains, not consumed by insects, mice, or other roving predators, now clung in desperation to their supports.

"I thought you were taking care of this place, David. It looks like it could use a little TLC, don't you think?"

"I'm just following Maggie's instructions. She wants it left alone. She wants it left just like it was. Come on, I'll take you inside. She likes me to take a look inside from time to time just to make sure the critters haven't taken up full-time residency."

Turning the key in a large brass padlock on the hand-forged hasp, the rusted hinges creaked and groaned as the heavy planked door swung inward, announcing our presence.

"We need to take it a bit slow," David said. "You never know who else has decided to visit. A month ago I killed a six-foot rattler working on a nesting place just above the stove. Just before winter last year a mama skunk with her litter liked to give me the perfumed bath of my life when I looked in the bedroom without knocking. She had chewed her way in under the wall behind the bed."

Standing in silence, barely listening to David's story, I stood in awe, truly as if I were drifting back in time. Whoever had lived here certainly didn't show a propensity for modern comforts.

In the corner of the main living area stood a cast-iron potbellied stove perched atop a circle of river stones set to catch any errant sparks or falling embers. Barely visible was the word "Variety" cast into the feeder door above the spin draft.

In the kitchen next to a large cast-iron cook stove, its nickel trim now sporting some tarnish with age, stood a 1930s vintage Top Monitor refrigerator. Its chilling abilities, no longer operational, it now sat sadly alone in silence. What had once been modern technology, its dull porcelain finish with crowning coils atop the storage box now sat shrouded by a dusty piece of red plaid gingham.

Other than a few tables and chairs, the only two items of furniture left uncovered were a plank desktop mounted to the rear wall under the window and a settee positioned along a wall in the living room.

Like a beacon drawing my gaze to a far-off corner, my attention was suddenly captured by what appeared to be an 1800s vintage standing safe. Of all of the cabin artifacts, only this one item appeared to have been lovingly dusted or disturbed in any way.

Strange, with all the care it had been given to preserve its beauty, someone had gained access to it, not by combination, but by forced entry. Drill holes next to the safe's dial beneath the Gary Safe Company logo left no doubt thieves had done their dirty work here.

David had been checking to make sure all was secure in the bedroom as I knelt before the safe and slowly opened its partially ajar door that had once kept secure another's most valuable possessions…

"Stop!"

"Jesus Christ, David, you just scared the shit out of me. I was just curious about what the inside looked like!"

"That's one thing I never touch. Did you see it? There is one more under the cloth on the desktop."

"See what? Hell, man, when you shouted I thought I was about to be attacked by a snake or something."

"Don't touch them, but they're inside."

With my curiosity now piqued and with the light from the window illuminating its interior, I could see its contents.

"Feathers? You yelled at me about two feathers?"

"On the desk, there is another just like them," David said quietly.

A pair of what looked like eagle feathers, lovingly spread apart, but bound together by a beaded leather thong of rawhide, was all that remained in the safe.

"She never touches anything else in the cabin when she comes here. Sometimes she stays in here for hours, but it never appears that anything has been touched, except from time to time she moves the feathers. Her name is Maggie Rawlins. She's Dan and Hanna's daughter.

"Everything looks secure. Close the safe to leave it like it was and let's get out of here. Meet me around back and I'll lock up. I want to show you what's down by the creek."

Following David a few yards down the hill in the rear of the cabin, I suddenly felt the hair on the back of my neck stiffen, as if my body were telling me I was in imminent danger. I froze.

Slowly scanning the path for a possible snake–or worse–a large shadow engulfed me as a massive eagle swooped down from the treetops, his talons passing just inches from my scalp.

"*Help, David!*" I yelled, thinking I was being attacked and remembering he was the one carrying the gun.

"Relax. Just don't move. That's just Kato checking you out. I told you not to touch those feathers, didn't I? Kato has been living in the trees above the Rawlins place since before I moved here. He just wants to make sure you don't mess with the place, I guess. He won't do anything if he senses you're a friend." David stood silent for a moment. "Tell you what. We can come back down here later. I think maybe we'd better let Kato relax. He's not used to strangers roaming around here, especially a stranger that's been in the cabin and all. Let's go back to my place and have a couple of beers. I have something you might want to see. Besides, we haven't had any time just to sit and relax. I want to know what else you guys have been up to back in Oklahoma."

As I followed David back up the trail to the cabin, I paused briefly and looked back just to make sure Kato was satisfied with my retreat. There he was, all right, no longer in flight, but perched on the ridgeline of the roof. Wings spread slightly, slowly grooming his majestic chest feathers with his massive beak, while at the same time watching my every move, he appeared confident in the fact that he had established his dominance.

David and I spent the rest of the day mostly reminiscing about the good old days in Oklahoma when we had worked together in the construction field. David filled me in about what he had been up to around Riggins and the difficulties both he and Kris had encountered when they had moved to the area and tried to find work.

"I couldn't find a job around here to save my ass the first couple of years. It's still that way today for some of the new people who have moved to rural Idaho. Most of the jobs I could land were somewhat menial, some small carpentry or concrete stuff, but projects of any size were closely guarded by contractors who had established roots around this area.

"You know, Kris had taught school back home, but up around these parts, no way. Even if there had been an opening for a teacher, the best she was ever offered was a position as a substitute or as a teacher's aide, even if they had an opening for a full-timer. It took a few years, all right, but now things have changed. We're accepted as one of the locals. Everybody has to do their time, we figured.

"It really pissed both Kris and me off, and we held quite a bit of resentment at first, feeling that we were being snubbed, but after a little time passed, I guess we understood why they were standoffish. They were kind of like old Kato. This was their territory and we were invading it. It took a little time to convince them that we were not trying to take away their jobs and all. Work around here is and always has been cherished among the folk in small towns."

After a stroll down by the creek, David fired up his grill. It was coming on 4 o'clock, and as we stood by the flames of the ignited chunks of hardwood, out of the forest came the whinny of Molly, announcing Boyd's return.

"What say you two? Getting ready to burn a few steaks, are you? I sure hope you cut out a thick one for me there, David. I'm so hungry I was having thoughts of eating old Molly on the way back."

"How did it go up there, Dennis? Did you find any dopers?" David asked, obviously relieved that his friend hadn't come to any harm. Although it wasn't very common, a lawman venturing out in back country alone and nosing around where he wasn't welcome sometimes didn't end well.

Having heard about some of the stories of paramilitary groups locating to the rural parts of Idaho to escape the government's control, I, too, had harbored a few silent concerns for Boyd's safety when he had embarked on the scouting trip that morning.

"Nope, I didn't find any marijuana. I did come across some irrigation tubing and what looked like a place where someone had been probing around for a prime location to grow some, but nothing was there yet. With Molly's big old hoof prints now scattered all over the place, I think I might have spoiled their plans. They might realize that place they picked wasn't as isolated as they thought.

"Molly left them a couple of big piles of fertilizer, and I made it a point to leave plenty of boot prints. I also cut their tubing into several small pieces. For now I think I'll just let them know somebody was there. But enough about that, when's dinner?"

After enjoying one of the best barbequed steaks I had ever eaten, the three of us spent the rest of the evening just exchanging pleasantries. It felt good spending time with my old friend David, and I got the feeling that Dennis had truly accepted me as his friend as well.

After Dennis departed for town, David and I retreated to the back porch. In Dennis's absence, David now had something to add to what he had been on the verge of talking about earlier that day--the story behind the Rawlins's cabin.

"Kevin, Dennis gave me his nod of approval about you, so what I am about to show you won't come as a surprise to him, just in case something comes up in future conversations with him while you're here. Let me go get something you might like to see."

With a small lantern in hand, David headed over to the shed next to Molly's stall, and I could see in the dim light that he was moving some hay bales out from the front of what appeared to be a door. From behind the door he retrieved a package.

Tucking the package under his arm, he turned, and his gait took on a somewhat serious posture as he headed back to where I was sitting.

"Here, Kevin. Since you're an old story teller and seem to be so curious about that cabin, I have something here that you might like to read while you're staying with us. It's something that Dan Rawlins had written and asked me to give to Maggie the day he went away.

"When Maggie left the place after Dan was given up for dead, she brought it over to me and asked me to keep it safe for her just in case she ever needed it. Besides Maggie, only Dennis, Kris, and I know of its existence, and now you do as well."

Gently, I unfolded the two layers of oilcloth that were protecting the contents. Inside was a leather pouch that contained what appeared to be hand-written pages almost three inches thick. The name Maggie Rawlins was lovingly tooled into the leather on the front of the pouch.

"It's about the family, Kevin. Dan knew he was going to die, and he didn't want to leave this world with Maggie not knowing the truth about her life. He'd told me on more than one occasion about his and Hanna's childhood when they had been orphaned. How Hanna had always worried that something might happen to them and then Maggie wouldn't know the real truth about her past. Even though we had become good friends with Dan and Hanna almost immediately, the story was quite revealing to Kris and me when we read it."

A strange feeling suddenly came over me as I was handed what was obviously, a hand written journal of the Rawlins family's lives.

"David, are you sure I should be reading this? I'm not sure...."

"Kevin, if you knew Dan Rawlins like I did, he would be proud that you would take the time to read what he wrote. If I didn't know you like I do, I wouldn't have let you see it in the first place. You may just find some things in his writings that may explain a few things. Like the eagles you told me about earlier today, the ones up at Windy Gap, maybe even a few interesting things about old Kato."

Now finding myself filled with the adrenalin of the day, I laid awake as David retired for the evening. Unable to get the vision of the Rawlins cabin out of my mind, I retrieved Daniel Rawlins's journal that was beckoning my attention. An eagle's cry suddenly broke the silence of the night as I opened the leather pouch. Turning to the first page I felt a feeling of warmth flow though me as I suddenly realized that this destination wasn't of my planning at all, my presence here this night was meant to be. Something or someone, perhaps a higher power had guided me to this place, not for fishing or to rekindle an old friendship, but for a very special purpose, it was the journal. I then began to read the words left behind by Daniel Rawlins.

"To my precious Maggie...."

Chapter 2

I had learned that David and Kris had only known Dan and Hanna for two years before Hanna passed. David explained that both Dan and Hanna were descendants of the Nez Perce Indians. David said that Dan had commented many times about the Nez Perce customs and how they continued to intrigue him.

It had not been a surprise to either David or Kris, that Dan and Hanna's genetics had played a major role in the life the couple had lived. A life of devotion to family as well as their love of nature had also been noticeably present. David and Dan had become good friends almost immediately after they had met. Both had held a deep sense of not only love and devotion for family, but the love of hunting and fishing as well, and that is where their close friendship had first begun.

David had come across the carcass of an elk shot out of season. The shooter had simply killed a large bull elk for his horns. Dan had been out scouting the area when he had encountered David on the trail en route to town to report what he had found.

Bonded by their disdain for anyone who would not only kill this animal illegally but commit such an act of wanton waste of its meat was incomprehensible. Knowing that time was of the essence, based on the freshness of the kill, the two of them joined forces and began to track the perpetrator.

With the combination of their keen knowledge of hunting and tracking, as well as their knowledge of the local terrain, it didn't take long before the two of them were hot on the trail of their suspect. In less than an hour, two miles from the kill site, they found them.

Their tracks drag marks, and a sporadic blood trail had led them to a box canyon far off the beaten track where a logging road ended. Watching from the tree line, they spied two men, their clothing bloodied, straining to load the big bull's antlered head into the back of an old pickup truck.

"Stop right there! Sheriff's Department!" Dan shouted, giving authority to his order.

Hidden in the shadows, the two men had the advantage over this duo who now found themselves trapped in a dead end. Faced with a decision to fight or attempt to flee, the two men cowered and complied with Dan's stern orders.

"Both of you, move back from the truck and lie on the ground. Do anything but what I tell you to do, and by God Almighty, it will be the last thing you ever do. I'll blow your heads off!"

Dan immediately recognized the taller of the two as Brady Scruggs, a known poacher, a well-known braggart, and local drunk. He had been suspected of killing out of season multiple trophy elks and buck deer for their head mounts. It was rumored that he would hide the heads in a cold storage somewhere on the Indian reservation, then when the legal season was about to end, he would market his wares to unsuccessful hunters.

Befriending them with offers of alcohol and sympathetic affirmations about their skills, Scruggs would blame an unsuccessful hunt on harsh regulations or mismanaged game herds. If he could find a fool to buy into his rant, someone who had the money to do so, Scruggs would provide the hunter with a trophy for a price to fill his tag so the hunter could brag to his friends back home about his big hunt.

Dan and David bound the men's hands, and after a quick pat down for any hidden weapons, stepped a few paces back and ordered both poachers to their feet.

Immediately Scruggs recognized Dan. "You ain't no God Damn police! You got no damn business here at all. Take these damn straps off our hands, you God Damn do-gooding nosey bastards."

Unnoticed by David, while Scruggs continued to rant at Dan, Dan was slowly unbuttoning his woolen shirt to reveal his Deputy Sheriff's badge dangling from a small chain around his neck.

Smiling, Dan retorted, "That's the second big mistake you made today, Scruggs, you worthless bastard! Sorry about this, David. I guess I forgot to tell you that from time to time I help out Dennis down at his office. If you don't mind, though, let's just keep this little badge thing between the two of us. As you can see, I don't like to advertise it if I don't have to."

David, as shocked as the two culprits, didn't even consider asking any questions. "Your business is your business there, Dan. I didn't hear or see a thing."

"Raise your right hand, David, and repeat after me. I, David Freeman, solemnly swear to uphold the law, to keep silent about doing it when I say it is necessary, and to shoot either one of these bastards right between the eyes if they say one more word that takes God's name in vain."

Somewhat bewildered, but having full trust in Dan, David just smiled and raised his palm and responded loudly, "I do Sheriff!"

Because of David's timely discovery and Dan's care to preserve the initial kill scene for evidence, and coupled with their quick action to track these two while the kill was fresh, a follow-up investigation by the Idaho Fish and Game Department recovered enough evidence to prosecute Brady Scruggs and his accomplice.

Although Scruggs's assistant received probation, loss of his weapons, a ban on hunting in Idaho for life, along with a stiff fine for the event that took place that day, he was ultimately relieved when he learned of his partner's fate.

The prosecution of Scruggs resulted in an indictment on thirty-seven felony counts, landing Brady Scruggs in the care of the Idaho Department of Corrections for fifteen years and a fine of $50,000.00.

Armed with a search warrant for Brady Scruggs's cabin and barn, Fish and Game recovered multiple examples of Scruggs's poaching, along with several stolen rifles, handguns, and a small cache of explosives that Scruggs had been rumored to have used for trophy trout and salmon fishing.

From that day forward, animal poaching in the area became almost nonexistent, and an unbreakable bond of friendship between David and Dan had been formed. A short time later, Dan had offered the property next to his place for David and Kris to build their cabin. The rest, David would say, is history.

David spoke of how it had been about two years after they moved next to the Rawlins place that Kris had noticed that Dan's wife Hanna just didn't seem to be acting like she normally did.

Even though both of the women lived close to one another, it was seldom that they spent much time together during the daytime. Other than a smile or a wave to one another, very different interests separated the two. What they did have in common was their concern for each other's safety, both often finding themselves alone back in this reclusive, forested setting. It was quite common for both of these women to keep a sharp eye out. Though subtle, like the wildlife in the area, each of them had developed a keen sense of awareness and became cautious when anything around them seemed out of the norm.

Kris had mentioned to David that she had noticed Hanna's daytime strolls on the property, spending the cool morning hours tending her vegetable garden, or just doing routine everyday chores around the cabin, had suddenly, for no apparent reason, stopped.

She would see Hanna down behind the cabin for hours on end just sitting and staring toward the warm spring behind their cabin.

On more than one occasion Kris had approached Hanna and tried to find out if something was wrong, but Hanna would just smile, wave her off, and say that sometimes she just got lonesome with Maggie now gone off to college.

Although David and she had never had any children, Kris understood. She lived far away from her family, so she often dealt with that type of loneliness. It must be a very emotional thing for Hanna, she thought. Maggie had been her life, her companion on those lonely nights when Dan had been gone on his trips.

Dan, however, being much closer to the situation, had noticed that Hanna would fall into bouts of deep depression for days on end. He made mention of this in confidence to David. Dan also had assumed initially that Hanna's depression was the result of Maggie's absence. But when the night sweats and nausea began to appear on a more frequent basis, coupled with the spells of depression, Hanna's physical condition was now becoming a very serious issue. The excuses that Hanna came up with to explain her physical troubles were no longer excuses Dan was willing to accept.

The final straw came one afternoon when she became violently nauseous while Hanna and Dan had been in town shopping. Her excuse that time was that she had eaten something that didn't agree with her the day before.

But Dan, on the other hand, knowing that they had been together almost continually for the past two days and had consumed the same foods, coupled with her inability to make eye contact with him when the questions arose, knew she was lying.

One morning Dan had gone into wake her, and found her tucked tight in a fetal position, her head resting helplessly in a pool of vomit. He panicked. There would be no more excuses; it was time to intervene.

Wrapping her in a quilt, he cradled her limp body in his arms. His eyes welling with tears, his strength and courage nearly failed him. He now had to muster every bit of his internal strength just to walk.

"I'm taking you to see Doc, Hanna. I have you now. I promise everything is going to be okay. Please Hanna. I need you to help me, baby. Hold on, sweetheart. Everything is going to be okay, I promise." Her blank stare and dilated pupils gave little doubt, that Hanna's condition was now critical.

Her shallow breathing and elevated temperature screamed out to him that the body of his beloved Hanna was being ravaged by some unknown vicious demon. He could see that she was trying to move her lips to cry out to him for help, but the only sounds she could make were barely audible whimpers.

Dan raced into town with Hanna wrapped in blankets in the back of the jeep. As Dan sped by, Boyd was engulfed in a huge cloud of dust; he stood beside his vehicle on the dirt road along the river, issuing a citation to a tourist. Fearing something was wrong and abandoning the tourist, Boyd jumped into his cruiser, took up pursuit, and arrived in Riggins just as Dan skidded to a halt in front of Doc Morgan's office.

Oblivious to Boyd's presence, Dan bolted through the office door and yelled for the doctor. "Doctor Morgan has gone out on a house call," a young girl seated at the receptionist desk told Dan.

In a state of near panic, Dan whirled around mid-stride, stormed out, and raced back to the jeep. Hanna needed a doctor and she needed one *now*. Boyd paused just long enough to listen to Dan's brief explanation of what was going on, then immediately assisted in lifting Hanna's now almost lifeless body from the jeep. Together they loaded her into the rear seat of his patrol car.

Boyd grabbed for the police radio mike and began barking orders to the dispatcher. "Alert the highway patrol, Forest Service Ranger's Office, and the Emergency Room in White Bird that we're heading north from Riggins with a patient." With his red lights flashing and siren blaring to clear all traffic ahead, the three sped north through the center of this once sleepy river town.

Two hours later, Doc Morgan arrived at the hospital emergency room and located Dan. He'd heard the news from his receptionist. Taking charge of the situation, he ordered a staff nurse, "Administer a mild sedative to Dan here before I end up having to deal with two patients." He then retreated to the doctors' locker room, gowned, then headed into the surgical suite where a staff doctor was preparing Hanna for emergency surgery.

Several hours later, Doctor Morgan finally reappeared in the family waiting area, still gowned in surgical scrubs. His face was flushed. The redness in his eyes and the dark circles beneath them spoke volumes as he made his way slowly across the room.

"How's Dan doing, Dennis?" Doc asked.

"As good as can be expected, I guess. He won't eat or drink anything. He's just been sitting here silent as a tomb, staring at those damn swinging doors."

Slowly, Doc Morgan knelt in front of the chair where Dan sat trembling. "Is Hanna going to be okay, Doc? She's going to be fine, isn't she, Doc? She just has the flu, right?"

"Dan, you and Hanna are like family to me, and you know that. They had to do an emergency operation, but I was there the entire time. They're good doctors, I can promise you that." The doctor paused, and then cleared his throat. "They removed a large growth from her abdomen, and they're doing a biopsy in the lab right now. But Dan, I'm sorry. It doesn't look very good."

Holding both of Dan's hands like a caring father, Doctor Morgan began to softly explain that when the surgeon opened Hanna's abdominal cavity he found a cancerous growth that had appeared on her x-ray. The tumor that they had removed was somewhat larger than a grapefruit, and it was obvious that the cancer had spread to several of her other organs.

"But she is going to be all right isn't she, Doc?" Dan softly murmured, tears making their way down this battle-hardened soldier's cheeks.

"She is resting peacefully right now, son, but she's a very sick girl. She'll be out from the anesthesia for probably the next several hours. She's in the intensive care unit right now, so you won't be able to see her until she is stabilized. I'm going to stay with her until she wakes up. As soon as I find out the lab results, I'll let you know immediately.

"Daniel, I think you need to go with Dennis and get a motel room here in town. You shouldn't just sit here at the hospital. There's nothing you can do right now, and it could be several more hours before you'll be allowed to see Hanna. If you get a room at the motel it will be more comfortable and you'll be close by, just in case she needs you.

"If you want to help Hanna right now, I think you should try to get in touch with Maggie at school. I think she needs to come home as soon as she can arrange it. You need to be the hero right now for Hanna, the hero Hanna has told me she loves so much. She needs your courage now, Dan. She needs your courage now more than ever."

Even though Dennis tried to portray a positive attitude, his words of encouragement as they drove to the motel fell on deaf ears. As supportive as he was, Dennis knew in his heart that the news about Hanna was as devastating to Dan as a lightning bolt striking a large pine tree in the forest– a trunk-splitting strike that had rattled his friend from his crown to his roots.

For the next hour, Dennis assisted Dan by making call after call to various people at the University of Montana in Missoula, but to no avail. The University was on break, and the only people who may have had answers to any of his questions were either out of town or didn't have access to information about Maggie's whereabouts.

Just as they were about to abandon their search for Maggie, the telephone rang. Dan grabbed the receiver just as it rang the second time. "Yes it is. I'm Maggie's father."

Dennis stood by his side, impatiently waiting for any information that would allow him to muster his emergency police services to help his friend to reunite his family, but his wait was in vain.

"Thank you. If you hear from her or if you can get the message to her to call me back at this number, I would appreciate it, Sara. I know you've done all you could do." Slowly, Dan returned the receiver to its cradle, then shrugged his shoulders.

"She's in South America somewhere. She went with a group from the Forestry Department at school on a last-minute field trip down to the Amazon Rainforest to do research on clear cutting. Some other student backed out at the last minute, and Maggie took her place without even being able to contact us, I guess. The girl said that the last thing she had heard was that the group was in an encampment with a tribe of Indians known as the Yanomami. What in the hell is a damn Yanomami?" he suddenly screamed out in utter frustration.

"She'll call, Dan. They'll get in touch with her."

Darkness fell, and the sedative Doc had instructed Dennis to slip into a drink for Dan finally overcame Dan's tormented emotions and frustrations, casting him into a silent world known only to him. Assured that Dan had now drifted off in a drug-induced slumber, Dennis quietly slipped out of the room to a liquor store just a block away to obtain his own prescription to ease his nerves and help him get through the night ahead. What he needed now was a few stiff shots of Jack Daniels.

Sometime around midnight, Dennis was awakened by Dan's screams. He had expected that the haunting events of the day might invade Dan's mind, but these screams were nothing like what would be expected to come from a man's loving thoughts of his wife.

Profane rants of "I'll kill you, you son of a bitch!" and "Just shoot all six of them!" filled the darkness. Dan was in so much mental torment the Devil himself had stepped in to try to haunt

Dan's mind with God only knows what kind of memories he had managed to lock away deep in his subconscious. The dark vault in Dan's mind had somehow been opened, and the horrific events he had experienced during the war, now found their way to his lips.

"Wake up, Dan. Wake up. It's Dennis. You're okay, buddy. It's just a dream. *Wake up!*"

Startled, Dan suddenly awoke, his mind still fogged from sedation. "Jesus Christ. What the hell is happening to me? First I saw Hanna waving goodbye to me, then there was gunfire everywhere."

Dan's eyes began to fill with tears, and Boyd understood that the time for any chance of rest had passed.

"I think we need to run over to the hospital and check on Hanna, don't you, Dan?"

Doc's suggestion of the motel might have been a good one at the time, but now Dan needed to be close to Hanna. He needed to be anywhere but where Dennis had just snatched him back from.

Dan could do little more than wait. He'd done all he could to reach Maggie, but the organizers in South America said that getting the news to his daughter with any speed was nearly impossible. Authorities at the university advised that they would do their best to forward news of the situation, but the lines of communication with the field group were reported to be sporadic at best.

Hanna was stable but resting in a drug-induced coma when Dan entered her room. The multiple monitors, wires and tubes, feeding precious life into Hanna's frail, unresponsive body removed any doubt in his mind that his beloved wife was in an extremely critical condition.

The staff surgeon as well as an assisting hospital oncologist had determined that a hopeful prognosis of recovery for frail Hanna was unlikely, so Dr. Morgan arranged with the staff to make ready a comfortable resting area for Dan in her room. Through that day and the following night, Dan never left Hanna's bedside. At 5:38 the following morning, the hospital's emergency response team responded to an alarm emitting from Hanna's life support monitor. After assessing her for any remaining vital signs, they determined nothing more could be done. A physician slowly shook his head, removed a pen from his smock, and entered the time of death at 0551 hours. Hanna had never regained consciousness.

Now all that remained of Hanna was her love, delicately cradled in Dan Rawlins's heart. Bending ever so gently, Dan stroked her raven black hair away from her face and kissed her gently on the lips.

"Goodbye, my love. Blaze a trail for me to follow. I will look for you in the canyon of our ancestors. Your glowing halo will guide me."

Taking Dan's hand, a nurse, with tears glistening on her cheeks, reached forward and gently placed her other hand on Dan's face, turning his stare from the body of the beautiful Indian maiden that had been all that Dan had ever lived for.

"It's time, Dan. It's time to let her go. She is in God's hands. She needs to walk down the trail with Him. She'll be there waiting for you, Dan, and you will find her."

It was a few hours later before the emotional finality of the tragedy of Hanna's death slowly began to ebb. Dan, along with the support of his friends, Dennis and Doc, completed the legal formalities with the hospital and were provided a release for Dan to take possession of Hanna's body for the trip back to Riggins.

In the hallway outside Hanna's room, a nurse stood waiting as the three approached. Like a sentinel guarding the place where

Hanna's body lie, was the nurse who had comforted Dan at the time of her death.

Dressed, not in nursing scrubs with cap and mask, she now wore a simple beaded tunic made of softened deerskin. Her shoulder-length, raven-black hair that had earlier been hidden beneath her surgical cap was now held tightly to her head by a simple leather thong.

"Mr. Rawlins, I hope you won't think I am imposing. I took the liberty of helping prepare Hanna for her journey."

Slowly turning, the woman opened the door to Hanna's room.

"She is waiting for you to take her home, Mr. Rawlins."

Atop the bed lie the body of his beloved, fully encased in a magnificent hand-woven Nez Perce blanket. As Dan stepped closer to the bedside, he could see that a fold in the covering had been carefully turned back to reveal Hannah's sleeping face.

"I will never forget this wonderful gesture, miss." Dan told her, drawing from all the strength of his manhood to hold back new tears. "She looks just beautiful. Hanna would be very thankful for what you have done for both of us."

Not wanting to further delay, Doc intervened. "Nurse, if you would be so kind to summon someone with a gurney, I think it's time for us to leave."

Like the winds that frequented the canyons, the news of Hanna's passing became the buzz around town. Although she had spent most of her life on the outskirts of Riggins, it was evident that among several members of the community both Dan and Hanna had most definitely touched their hearts.

It was just after dark when Dan's jeep carrying Hanna's body arrived back at the cabin. David and Kris had learned of Hanna's death from a deputy that had stopped by Dan's cabin earlier that afternoon to drop off sympathy cards and food that had been brought by friends to the Sheriff's office in Riggins.

Dan carried Hanna's wrapped body into the cabin and placed her on their bed. In compliance with their Nez Perce traditions, Hanna would be laid to rest the following day. During the night, Dan lovingly stroked Hanna's body with warm damp cloths to cleanse her. With a makeup brush he covered her face with traditional red paint, dressed her in the same deerskin dress she wore the day they had been married, and wrapped her once again in the tribal blanket he had been given by the nurse at the hospital.

A few hours before dawn, David was awakened by the engine noise of the jeep as it drove off down the lane from the cabin. Taking forestry back roads known only by a few of the locals, forest rangers, and law enforcement personnel, Dan made his way into Hells Canyon to a clearing just below the top of She Mountain.

After digging a grave overlooking the Snake River valley, Dan removed his duster and retrieved Hanna's body, placing it upon a flat stone pinnacle just feet from the summit.

Building a small fire next to the stone, Dan stood facing Hanna, arms outstretched, and began to chant a mournful prayer toward the rising sun.

As if responding to Dan's funeral prayers to his ancestors' spirits, one by one the eagles came. Like a gathering of mourners dispatched by God Himself, within minutes more than twenty of the great eagles of the canyon took silent roost atop the stony ridge surrounding him. As if patiently and respectfully waiting to welcome a new angel to their numbers, these magnificent feathered creatures sat silently as Dan completed his prayer chant.

Slowly, Dan lowered his precious Hanna into her tomb of eternal sleep, when suddenly he appeared. From behind a rock outcropping, the Indian chief who had come to Hanna and Dan in the canyon years before, once again stood in front of both as if they were his children. Never saying a word, the old Indian reached out his hand and placed two large eagle feathers on Hanna's wrapped body, turned back toward the sun, and then vanished.

Then, one by one, the majestic eagle honor guard dipped their white-feathered crowns toward Hanna's grave, then vaulted skyward. Higher and higher they rose on the warm thermals of Hanna's burial fire, one by one silently disappearing into the heavens above.

Two weeks passed before Dan received a telegram from his daughter Maggie. She had written only that she had been told there had been an emergency and that she needed to come home as soon as possible. She wrote that she would be flying back from South America on the 18th, just three days away, and would be arriving at the airport in Boise on American Airlines on the 19th at 6:00 p.m.

Chills ran down Dan's spine when the plane pulled up to the terminal. Halfway down the jet way he saw her, and tears began to well in his eyes.

"Daddy, where is Mama? Is she okay? The school chaplain sent a message for me at the village where we were and told me there was an emergency, but not what it was. Is Momma sick?"

Reaching out, Dan took Maggie into his arms and hugged her. He knew she could see the tears in his eyes, but he couldn't form the words to answer her question. As he slowly released her and she pulled back to ask again, he found the courage to answer.

"Your Momma passed away, baby. Hanna is gone!"

Gasping for breath, her knees went weak, and before Dan could react, Maggie fainted, collapsing to the floor in front of several people waiting for other arriving passengers. Airline staff and two security officers helped Dan move Maggie into a private security room where she slowly regained consciousness. After several tense moments, Dan managed to calm everyone down and was granted his request for a few moments of privacy for them both to regain their composure.

On the three-hour drive back to Riggins, Dan filled Maggie in on all the details of the events that had led up to Hanna's death. He had assured Maggie that with the type of cancer and the extent of its insidious, aggressive progression throughout her organs, there was nothing the doctors could do to save her. God had spared her mother. He had taken away her pain and had given her eternal peace. She would no longer suffer.

The following morning, Dan drove Maggie up into the canyon to visit her mother's gravesite. Recent rains and strong winds had already shifted the freshly turned soil; it had begun to return to its original form. The slight mound had settled into the hillside, and new shoots of spring grasses had already begun to take root. Only the remnants of a bouquet of wilted wildflowers Dan had left behind gave evidence that the grave had ever existed.

Maggie stayed on at the cabin for another five days before they both decided that it would be best for her to return to the University. Except for Dan, there was nothing left to keep her in Riggins.

Chapter 3

It had now been almost five years since Hanna had passed. Maggie and Dan still kept in touch, but their relationship was not nearly as close as it had been when Hanna was alive.

Maggie had graduated from college and was working with the Boise Cascade Lumber Company in their corporate office in Seattle, Washington. She had still not married, but she had a fiancé named Ted Sterling, another kid with a degree in forest management.

Although Ted had come to Riggins on a couple of visits when he and Maggie had first gotten together, Dan could never figure out what it was Maggie saw in this man to make her want to marry him. Although he had always been cordial in his conversations with Ted, behind his pleasant façade, Dan had noted an attitude of boastful arrogance. But thinking maybe he was just being a typical father, he tried to dismiss those negative feelings for Maggie's sake.

Ted's family had been in the lumber business for generations, but as a young man he had spent most of his days rafting on the rivers and enjoying the fruits of the families' wealth. Like Jiminy Cricket, Ted had spent most of his life fiddling around and playing with the girls, while his father and two brothers had toiled in the forest and built the families' business.

Regardless of Dan's personal opinions about Ted's character, he did not outwardly oppose Maggie's choice for a future husband. Ted may have displayed a sheepskin diploma on the wall from a university that pronounced him a forester with a successful business future ahead, but in Dan's opinion, Ted had as much of a chance nurturing a redwood or ponderosa pine to grow as a mosquito would have bringing down one of the mighty eagles of Hells Canyon. His education that he continually boasted about, may serve him well in deciding which trees needed to be cut for lumber, but his true knowledge of how to grow new forests had always seemed to Dan to be lacking. In Dan's mind, Ted might be better suited growing weeds than mighty forests.

But this was Maggie's life, not his, and Hanna and Dan had always wanted only happiness for their daughter. If Ted made Maggie happy, so be it.

It had been a long day. It was time to brush old Molly's tired back and give her a healthy ration of her favorite oats. Annie, Dan's Beagle dog, waddled around the corner of the cabin, fresh from her favorite napping place on the back porch, and greeted Dan with a lick to his hand and a flurry of wags from her white-tipped tail.

Although the years had taken a toll on her now sagging bellied body, in her heart Annie still tried to act like a puppy any time Dan made an appearance at the end of his work day.

"Have a good night, Molly. Me and Annie here are going to go in and burn a nice steak. Don't let that old nighttime bogeyman get you, girl. We'll see you in the morning."

Finishing supper, Dan took a stroll down to the warm spring behind the cabin. Resting his tired muscles and bones in its medicinal, swirling waters had become one of the few things left, besides Molly and Annie, which he truly derived pleasure from.

Since Hanna's death, the thought of his own passing had been a constant reminder that both their parents had died without Dan and Hannah knowing their parents' past. He realized he and Hanna had shared very little of their own pasts with Maggie, so for Maggie's sake, that night Dan made the decision to write a journal for Maggie, a journal that would reveal things that had been kept secret from her, a journal that would explain some of the mysteries of their lives.

Most importantly, Maggie was now a grown woman, and it was time she learned one of the most important secrets that had been kept from her. Though they'd nurtured and loved their daughter from babyhood to adulthood, she needed to be told the secret: She would always be the daughter who bore their name and their love, but she could never be the daughter of their blood.

A warm glow filled the small pine log cabin from a coal oil lamp perched on the shelf above Dan Rawlins's desk. Although he did have electricity, he always enjoyed watching the lamp's flame dance in the surrounding darkness. Dawn was just about to break over the mountains off to the east of the Salmon River on the 28th of June. This would be a special day for Dan. Today was his birthday.

He had been awake since 3:00 a.m. This was the third night in a row pain had shaken him from his slumber. A recurring, pulsating, dull ache deep within his lower back and gut had robbed him of the sleep he so desperately sought. For almost a year he had been experiencing the symptoms of severe indigestion that had first emerged on a hunting trip off Highway 12 near Lolo Pass.

At first Dan had thought that his age or the hundreds of miles he had spent on his loyal mule Molly's back were finally beginning to take their toll on this saddle-worn cowboy. His insatiable appetite for adventure, as well as his years of countless trips up the mountainsides and down the rugged canyons of Northern Idaho, were now becoming more than he could handle.

For the past few months, his bowels had been producing light clay-colored, odorous stools, unlike anything he had ever experienced. Further, his daily morning stretch, which in the past had loosened his muscles as he rose from a ground- laid bedroll, now only exacerbated the dull pain haunting his belly and lower back. Saddling Molly or loading packs on his other mules in preparation for one of his trips became all he could physically bear.

Two weeks ago he had made a trip into Riggins to see his friend, Dr. Morgan. To diagnose Dan's symptoms, Doc had sent some blood work, along with a few other tests, to a lab in Lewiston for analysis.

If your medical situation required absolute discretion, Doc was truly one you could count on for silence. Dan considered Doc a trusted friend and wonderful town doctor, but at seventy years of age, he didn't quite trust him enough to properly diagnose his gastrointestinal problems. A few stitches on the head was one thing; a visit from one of Doc's gloved hands to his backside was something totally different. Dan had previously allowed Doc to probe his body on only two other occasions. The first was to remove a bullet fragment from Dan's upper right thigh, shortly after Hanna had given him a prized antique Colt .45 Peacemaker revolver on his 40th birthday.

Like any old cowboy, Dan just had to try his hand at fast draw. What's a gunslinger to do if he can't show off his skills to his little lady by demonstrating a blazing draw of a six gun in the unlikely event an outlaw showed up at the cabin? Well, unfortunately, when Dan drew his weapon with lightning speed; he accidentally discharged a round into a cast iron skillet hanging from a crossbeam on the back porch.

Although it hadn't been his intended target, his trusty Colt discharged a lead 250 grain bullet square into the edge of that skillet. The bullet ricocheted, landing deep into Dan's thigh, right next to his fast-draw holster.

When Dan realized the slug's removal would require a bit more than his first-aid skills and nerves could handle, Hanna called for Doc Morgan. When Doc arrived, it was all the two of them could do to stifle their laughter over the old "Dan Skillet Shootout." Dan's ego had taken a far worse beating than the superficial wound had done to his leg.

Cowboy Dan stood in the front doorway sporting a splint on his right upper leg. With his gun belt removed, he looked like a little boy waiting to have to tell his mother that he'd just shot out a window with his new Red Rider BB gun.

When Doc arrived to tend to the injury, he just couldn't resist a little hazing.

"Howdy, Marshal," Doc quipped. "I understand you had a shootout with that outlaw Black Skillet, and kilt him dead."

Not wanting to show Doc his embarrassment, Dan jibed back, "Yep. Sure did, Doc. I gave old Black Skillet every opportunity to surrender. He was quick, but I was quicker. I saw it in his eyes. He was gonna draw on me, and…."

"Oh, shut up and sit down and let me get the damn slug out!" Doc interrupted what he knew would be a lengthy recitation of pure bullshit from his friend. He had other patients in town that needed his attention far more than Dan needed an audience.

"Drop your pants and sit down! I have better things to do than waste my time listening to your heroic bullshit! Just keep this clean and change the bandage before it gets real filthy like the rest of you. Come by and see me in a few days and I'll check it again to make sure I don't have to cut off that holster leg of yours."

A few months later, Doc had to be summoned back to the cabin a second time for an unusual emergency. This time, Dan had gone to Missoula, Montana, to pick up a new saddle he had ordered for Molly, and to meet with a man to discuss a fall elk hunt.

The man he met just happened to have a litter of Beagle pups turning six weeks old. Cowering in the corner of the kennel, atop a clump of straw, sat the runt of the litter-- a little lemon colored female just half the size and lighter in color than the others.

Looking up at Dan, she whimpered softly like a scared little girl, fleas racing across her slender snout, mercilessly biting her tender muzzle. Instantly, she stole Dan's big heart.

That afternoon, Dan couldn't wait to show off his new prize he had named Annie to Hanna and his trusty mule Molly. Dan called toward the house, summoning Hanna, then headed to the stable where Molly was feeding on her bag of oats.

"Hey, Molly, old girl, look at what I got he–"

Before Dan could finish forming the word "here," this little Beagle ball of fire let out a howl that could be heard by her brothers clear back to Montana. Leaping from Dan's arms, she headed straight for the biggest rabbit she had ever seen…Molly!

Old Molly did what she was told, all right. Without missing a chew, she turned her gaze toward Annie who was heading directly for her rear hoof. Calmly, without even blinking, Molly drew her leg back, cocked, and fired. Molly's aim was perfect, as always–a direct hit. Her left hoof landed right under Annie's jaw, sending the little attack dog through the air on the ride of her life.

"Molly! What the hell is the matter with you? She's just a puppy, damn you!"

The truth of the matter was, Molly not only didn't like dogs that much, she didn't particularly like to be scolded for delivering what she considered a reasonable nudge to this errant little mutt.

Witnessing the confrontation, Hanna headed straight for this little yelping puppy sprawled on the ground. Dan continued his rant and headed for Molly. Molly knew Dan sometimes had a temper and a tendency to slap a mule hard on the ass, so she decided it was time to stand her ground for what she thought was right.

Like a lightning bolt from heaven above, Dan never even saw them coming. Stars swirled around in his head as Molly let Dan have it with both rear barrels. Hanna looked up just in time to see Dan do an acrobatic flip backwards into the wood pile and land in a heap.

After wetting his face with a cool cloth and gently nudging him, Hanna was able to bring Dan back to consciousness.

"Hanna, go get me my damn shotgun; I'm gonna shoot that sonofabitchin mule right square in the ass!"

Having a sweet spot in her heart for Molly, Hanna ignored the order for the shotgun and helped Dan to his feet. With his temper still boiling, Dan began to move forward, but once again went sprawling face first, this time in the dirt.

In all of the commotion, neither Hanna nor Dan had noticed the piece of a pine limb sticking out of the left side of his buttocks, the consequence of his impromptu tumbling act.

As before, Hanna summoned Doc and requested he make a house call so his friend's reputation as a tough cowboy would remain intact. With a shot of Jack Daniels for Doc and a shot of Meperidine in Dan's rear, Doc's skilled, nimble fingers eased the four-inch piece of pine branch from Dan's gluteus maximus. Seven stitches later, Dan's rear was repaired, but nothing could be done to cure Dan's embarrassment.

"Now for you, "little lady, Doc cooed, taking Annie in his arms. "It's your turn!"

With great tenderness, Doc gently cradled Annie to his chest and administered a puppy-sized dose of sedative. Then, with a few swipes of a razor on her furred, bruised muzzle to expose the small wound on her lower jaw, he sewed two quick stitches and Annie was good as new.

"Okay, now, Mr. Rawlins, this is your final warning. Skillet killing is something I can turn a blind eye to, but animal abuse is another matter entirely. I just can't abide it." Giving Hanna a smile and a wink, he packed up his satchel and headed for the door, pausing a moment to write a prescription for pain pills. Although the pills were really for Dan, Doc just couldn't resist. "Hanna, dear, give one of these pills to Annie three times a day as needed for pain and a nice fresh bone once a day so she can exercise her jaw. Don't hesitate to call me if she has any trouble sleeping. Now, Dan, on the other hand, won't need anything for his pain. If he feels sore, just have him walk down the hill and soak his butt in the creek."

Walking past Molly on the way to his pickup, Doc patted the thousand-pound mule gently on her haunches and quipped, "Just remember who buys you those oats, old girl."

Dan smiled as he cleaned up the kitchen area, then sat back down at his desk to finalize his thoughts. He would write some of the events of the happier days when his dear Hanna's voice had warmed his heart in this special place. His mind wandered toward the pool....

Black of night gave way as dawn began to illuminate the small creek just beyond the rear porch of the cabin. A faint mist slowly began to appear upstream from a hot spring feeding the creek. Warmed by the depths of the earth, a fissure had opened centuries ago, creating a pool of steaming water– just one more of God's perfect creations. A natural hot tub to soothe a tired man's bones. Hanna had so loved this place. Dan remembered how she had looked like an angel when she would bathe their baby Maggie in this very spot.

It seemed like an eternity ago. Maggie was now a grown woman, and Hanna, his sweet love Hanna, now lay with her ancestors at peace. Caressed no longer by the loving arms of Dan, her spirit and loving heart now caressed only by the wistful breezes of angels wings in a place called Seven Devils. Strange he thought how this beautiful portal to Heaven, Seven Devils, could be such a frightening yet whimsical metaphor that only God's humor could have ever suggested.

Chapter 4

"*Migisi*" was the name Hanna's mother had given her when she had been born in the canyon of the Devils. Meaning *eagle* to the native Indians, the name couldn't have been more appropriate for one so beautiful and kind.

Dan had first met Migisi when he had returned from the East. He had been released from three years of military service in the Army, and now had a job waiting in White Bird, Idaho, where he had lived as a boy. He was to meet with the Sheriff of Idaho County, a man named Robert Grimsley, whom he had known while serving overseas.

Before his 9:00 a.m. meeting that morning, Dan had gone to the restaurant where he had only planned to relax with a cup of fresh coffee. As he looked up from reading the Idaho County paper, *The Free Press,* their eyes locked. Her eyes were as brown as the canyon walls, and her raven-black hair, cut just above her bronze shoulders, framed a face whose beauty was unrivaled by any other woman he had ever seen.

"Ah…coffee… I mean coffee please…. Dang, may I please… may I have a cup of coffee, miss?" Dan stammered, trying to find words to camouflage his awkwardness.

Turning away, she reached for the pot, then looked back over her shoulder and flashed Dan a broad smile. "My name is Hanna, and yours would be?"

Dan's lips again took on a mind of their own as he quickly stammered with a slightly raised voice, "Dan Rawlins, miss... I mean Daniel... jeez, I mean Dan or Daniel or either one would be great!"

He sounded like a fool. He heard snickers from other patrons behind him. He took a deep breath, placed his palms firmly on the counter, and waited for her return.

Placing his coffee in front of him, she followed the first with a more reserved smile. "Will you be wanting anything else, Mr. Dan or Daniel or Mr. Rawlins?"

Flushed with embarrassment like a schoolboy turned down by a girl at his first dance, Dan quickly downed the steaming hot brew, almost searing his throat, and laid a five dollar bill on the counter. He stood up.

Mumbling his thanks, he bowed his head and examined the floor. So not to have to see the delight on the faces of the other diners who had just witnessed this broken rooster having his tail feathers plucked out by a mischievous hen, he quickly made his way to the exit.

"Oh, Daniel, I hope I will see you again soon,"she called after him.

Not wanting to risk any further blunders, Dan turned and waved at her, then headed for his truck. This was not the time to rush forward; it was a time to retreat and formulate a plan. Next time he would do things right. Next time he would capture the heart of this angel he knew had to be his.

Two weeks later, Dan's manhood and confidence had sufficiently healed. He was ready to make another trip from Riggins back to the White Bird Diner. Through his binoculars, from a position he had taken up across the street, Dan watched Hanna serving a customer seated at the counter inside the restaurant. He waited for a space to clear at the counter, then crossed and made his entrance.

This time, after several refills of coffee, Dan finally managed to deliver what was about to be the speech that would change his life forever. As she stood before him, he slowly stood, placed his hat over his heart, and looked directly into her eyes.

"Miss Hanna, I would truly be honored if you would consider going with me this Saturday to the dance social they're holding at the White Bird Elk's Lodge. Of course, that is if you haven't already been invited by someone else, like a boyfriend, maybe?"

"Daniel, I would like that very much. I was hoping you might ask me, since I don't have a boyfriend and all."

Dan stared at Hanna's plastic White Bird Diner name tag resting on his desk. God, he missed her so. She'd been gone five years now.

For the next six months, whenever Dan was in town, the two had been almost inseparable. Hanna moved down to Riggins and found a job as a housekeeper at a small family-owned motel at the edge of town. With winter approaching, the vacancy rate was low, so the owners were kind enough to let her stay in one of the rooms as an extra boon to her small wages.

When the winter weather permitted, Dan had been helping out with maintenance on some of the campgrounds and Forest Service trails up in Hells Canyon, and when he and Hanna weren't together, he spent the rest of his time working on a project east of town on the Salmon River. As payment for his service, Dan told Hanna that the ranger had given him permission to stay in an old cabin back in the forest.

Although Hanna had been pressuring Dan to take her to this cabin where he stayed, he had always managed to create one story or another about how the place was in real bad, almost falling-down condition. He informed her that he would take her out to see it when he had completed the work he was doing on it, and not one day sooner.

It was now nearing spring, and the towering, majestic, snow-covered mountains were slowly awakening, beginning to prepare for another throng of flatlanders to enter their realm and explore their beauty.

For the next few weeks, Dan had heard the unmistakable sounds from the awakening forest, the occasional dying screams of a bawling deer fawn or elk calf as they fell victim to a marauding pack of hungry wolves, or the eerie screams of winter-starved cougars as they hunted for food to feed their spring litters.

A pair of bald eagles nesting high in a pine tree next to his cabin took to flight above him to gather salmon and trout from the rivers just a few miles away. Strange, he thought. Why had they chosen this place to nest, so far from the heights of the cliffs overlooking the river? Whatever the reason, his eagles were caring for two hatchlings, and it was spring.

Maybe they had befriended him because, throughout the winter months, he had provided those scraps of meat and a few extra fish that he had caught. Just a small gesture of kindness to ease their burden when the weather was so unforgiving. Maybe they felt a sense of protection around Dan. They had watched him from their high perch as he hunted game for food while leaving them totally unmolested. Maybe they somehow knew that he was a part of the makeup of their souls. The ancient blood of the Nez Perce, for whom the eagle was sacred, ran through his veins. By his mere presence in this land, he was bound by blood to protect them. It was time to make good on his promise to Hanna, to show her what he had accomplished.

It was early morning when Dan knocked on Hanna's motel room door. "Come on, sleepyhead, I have something to show you today. Get up now. We have lots to do today, and you're holding up the mules!"

"Mules? Just where do you think you're taking me, Dan Rawlins? You live in a cabin where you have to ride a mule to get there?"

"Not exactly, darlin. I just thought we could do something special before I show you the cabin, if that's all right. Put on some boots and jeans and get on out here. It's a beautiful morning."

Parked out front behind Dan's truck was a four-stalled horse trailer marked U.S. Forest Service, and standing inside were four of the largest chestnut-colored mules Hanna had ever seen.

"When I told Jim Baker up at the Forest Service Office that I was taking you up to Hells today he asked me if I would take some of his girls up to Windy Gap and corral them for him. The rangers are going up to the canyon in a few days, and he just wanted the animals to get acclimated to the elevation." This assured Hanna that his cabin was somewhat less remote. Dan had prepared a picnic basket for a trail lunch, and with Hanna's somewhat reluctance, they headed south to the dirt road that led to the top of the mountain and the trailhead.

Saddling two of the mules who had the best temperament and corralling the others, Dan, with Hanna in tow, headed down the narrow forest trail leading to the He and She Devil peaks.

On the western face of the mountain the snow had all but vanished, as the leeward face had given way to the winds of the Pacific. The sky of brilliant blue came alive with soaring birds as those that hadn't already nested searched for just the right bunting to adorn nests that would protect their soon-to-be-born hatchlings.

Sara and Trudy, the massive mules, picked their way gingerly as they descended the narrow trail, their plate-size hooves giving off a sucking sound as they lifted their pads from the muddy earth beneath them. Gone now were the conflagrations triggered by lightning from last summer's storms that had consumed this slope. The needles of the great pines that would normally silence their journey to visit the Devils had long since been reduced to ash.

As they cleared the burn area and ascended a trail crossing the remains of ancient rock formations, a valley of green lay before them, framing a cobalt abyss. This was their destination. This was one of God's chalices. This was Sheep Lake.

Near noon they reached Dan's planned destination, and the canyon had warmed to greet them. Spreading a quilt to protect themselves from the sprouts of the spring nettles, Hanna unveiled the lunch Dan had packed for them, as her suitor gazed off in the distance, humbled by the grandeur of their surroundings.

As Dan drew his attention back to this woman to whom he had given his heart, the sun crested the top of a far-off peak. Sunrays surrounded her in such an aura of purity and beauty, it did not ask, but demanded the magnificent surroundings to bow to her presence.

As their eyes met, a force flowed through their bodies, raising them both to their feet. Entwined as if Medusa herself had released her serpents, with every part of their souls now melting in God's crucible of love, they became one.

Chapter 5

That afternoon Dan and Hanna opened up to one another as they had never done before. Hanna revealed that she had not been a stranger to the Seven Devils. Her mother had been a member of a Nez Perce tribe whose village had been located somewhere in the canyon along the Snake River.

She faintly recalled that her mother and she had lived together in a town called Lewiston. She remembered her mother as very kind and loving, and proud that she and Hanna were of Indian blood, and that her mother had named her *Migisi,* an Indian name meaning eagle, after the beautiful birds that lived in the canyons.

Hanna's mother had told her about the old Nez Perce legend when she was about four years old. One of her fondest memories, her mother had talked about the tall mountain peaks and how they had come to exist.

"I don't remember the legend exactly," Hanna told Dan, gazing off toward He Devil Peak.

"But it went something like this, the best I can recall.

"Long ago, when the world was young, seven giant brothers lived in the mountains. The giant monsters were taller than the tallest pines and stronger than the strongest oaks.

"The ancestors feared these brothers because they ate children. Each year the brothers traveled eastward and ate all the little children they could find. The mothers fled with their little ones and hid them, but still, the giants ate so many, the headmen of the villages feared that the tribe would soon be wiped out. But no one was big enough or strong enough to fight the seven giants.

"The headmen of the tribe asked Coyote to help them. 'Coyote is our friend,' they said. 'He has defeated other monsters. He will free us from the seven giants.' Coyote agreed to help them; he would free the people from the seven giants.

"But Coyote did not know what to do so he asked the advice of his good friend Fox. 'We will first dig seven holes,' said Fox. 'We will dig them very deep, in a place where the giants will pass when they travel to the east. Then we will fill the holes with boiling liquid.'

"So Coyote called together all the animals who had claws–the beavers, the whistling marmots, the cougars, bears, rats, mice and moles–to dig seven deep holes. Then Coyote filled each hole with a reddish liquid. His friend Fox helped him keep the liquid boiling by dropping hot rocks into it.

"When it came time for the giants to journey eastward, they marched along, all seven of them, their heads held high in the air, sure that no one dared to attack them. Coyote and Fox watched from behind the rocks and shrubs.

"Down the seven giants tumbled into the seven deep holes of boiling liquid. They struggled and struggled to get out, but the holes were very deep. They fumed and roared and splashed.

"Then Coyote came out of his hiding place. The seven giants stood still. They knew Coyote.

"'You are being punished for your wickedness,' Coyote told the giants. 'I will punish you even more by changing you into seven mountains. I will make you very high, so that everyone can see you. You will stand here forever to remind people that punishment comes from wrongdoing. I will make a deep gash in the earth below you so that no more of your family can get across to trouble my people.

"Coyote caused the seven giants to grow taller, and then he changed them into seven mountain peaks. Then he struck the earth very hard so it opened up a deep canyon at the feet of the giant peaks.

"Now that is why the mountain peaks are called the Seven Devils. The Snake River filled the deep canyon, and the reddish copper ore scattered on the ground came from the splashing of the seven giants.

"It wasn't long after I turned four years old that the giants came for me. A woman and a man told me that my mother was gone and that I had to go with them. They put me in their car, and I remember crying for my mother, but I never saw her again.

"I was taken to a place called The Children's Finding and Aid Society in Lewiston. There they gave me the name Hanna, and told me that they were going to make my age five. They said my birthday would be the day they took me away, which was the first day of May. They were wonderful people, Dan. They weren't my family, but they took care of me and gave me a life."

As Hanna, with tears welling up in her eyes, turned back to Dan, he rose to his feet and looked down at her sitting like a child amongst the wildflowers.

"They took me as well, Hanna. They were not the same people, but I was taken just the same." Hanna wiped the tears from her eyes. "I don't remember my mother much at all. I was only four or five, I guess. I only remember the sounds of my father and mother yelling and fighting, and remember how I used to hide outside behind the house or barn, scared that they would hit me.

"I remember a policeman picking me up and taking me to a police station–at least I think that's where they took me–and then I don't remember much else except the first night at the orphanage. The place was called St. Joseph Mission School, located in Ashland, Montana.

"Mainly, the place was where they took Indian children that were either abandoned or had no one to care for them and no one who wanted them. I hated it, and I hated my mother and father for leaving me. I hadn't done anything wrong, but they gave me away.

"I never did find out why or whatever happened to my mother or father. They just disappeared from my life.

"I remember the spankings and the sounds of other girls and boys sometimes screaming and crying after we were sent to bed. Sometimes one of the priests would come for a girl or a boy after they turned the lights out, and then, after a short time you would hear them crying when they were brought back to the dormitory. When I got older I learned why they had been crying. They were being abused in unspeakable ways. God, I hated that place. And I hated God for sending me there. I had done nothing wrong except to be born.

"When I was around nine years old, I was terrified that someday they would come for me and I would be one of their victims, so I ran away. I hid in the back of a truck and ended up here in Idaho.

"I was in Riggins walking down the street one day when a sheriff stopped me and asked me where I lived. Having no answer and unable to give him anything but my first name, Daniel, and when I couldn't give him the names of my parents, I was caught. It didn't take long for him to figure out that I was a runaway, so eventually I was sent to the town of Orofino and placed in the Old State School there.

"The sheriff, who had found me, Mr. Jackson, kept in touch with me over the years. I guess he liked me. He would send me stuff for Christmas and sometimes boxes with clothes and candy and stuff. He wasn't married, so sometimes when he could get away he would come up to Orofino and visit me and take me fishing and hunting. The other boys would call me a snitch after he came to visit me once in his uniform.

"But I didn't care. They didn't know him like I did. He was just a good man, and he was my friend.

"When I turned seventeen he took me over to an Army recruiter in Missoula and helped me join the service. I guess he figured that it was a chance for me to get a good education and see the rest of the world. When I got out of the Army, Sheriff Jackson arranged a job for me back in Idaho, and the rest is history, you could say. He passed away from a heart attack two weeks after I returned to Riggins, and Rick Mears was his replacement."

When Dan finished, Hanna smiled. "It's been a beautiful day, Dan. You're very special, and I want you to know that. I have never opened up to anyone like I did to you today. I know how hard it is to look back, and I know how difficult it was for you to tell me what you just did. I'm sure it must have been just as painful for you as it was for me."

Dan's emotions began to show, so he quickly changed the subject. "If we don't get started back soon, we'll lose the sun by the time we get to the trailhead. We sure as heck don't want to have to search our way back in the dark."

The mules confidently carried Dan and Hanna back up the trail to Windy Gap. At the trailhead, Dan busted open a few bales of hay that would feed the animals for the next few days. After securing the four mules in the split-rail enclosure, they headed back down the winding seventeen miles into Riggins

With Hanna's head resting on Dan's shoulder, he decided that with all the emotions that had already surfaced that day, he would not subject his Hanna to any more surprises. Today's revelations had obviously taken their toll on her.

It had been a long day, a day of mixed emotions for both of them. He had planned to spend the day convincing Hanna that he, above all others, should be her choice as a lifelong companion. As they sat in the truck outside her motel, Dan stroked her hair gently and quietly began to speak.

"Hanna, it's been a wonderful day. I want you to know that I have deep feelings for you, and I hope you feel the same for me. I know you must be exhausted after our long day and what you felt you had to tell me, and I want you to know that I love you even more now having said what you did. I want you to get some rest, and if you still want to, I will come for you in the morning. I want you to see your cabin tomorrow. I want you to see with your eyes what you have done to my heart."

Hugging her closely to his chest, he whispered in her ear, "I want you to sleep well, my love, and dream happy dreams. I'll pick you up around 9:00 in the morning. I will show you then."

Dan escorted her to the door, and as Hanna was trying to absorb the words he had said, he kissed her on her forehead and said, "I love you *Migisi*, I love you, my little eagle." Then he turned and walked away.

"I love you, too, Dan Rawlins!" she shouted as he pulled away. "I love you, Daniel."

A grin found itself plastered across Dan's face as he headed south towards the cabin. He had heard Hanna's words as he'd pulled away from the motel. It was going to be a late night. He would shine and dust every corner of what was to be–he hoped–the gift he had prepared for this woman, the place they would start their new life together.

It was almost midnight before Dan stopped to survey his work. Each log next to the stove was not only of the same circumference but was the same length. He had painstakingly taken the time to make sure each object she cast her eyes upon would be perfect. From the lace curtains adorning the windows to the polished globes of the coal-oil lamps illuminating the room, had he missed anything? Quickly, his eyes scoured every corner of the cabin, just as his drill instructor had done when he had been in basic training.

He needed to add just one last thing. In a trunk at the foot of the bed lay a gift, wrapped in a white muslin cloth. He unbound the wrapping. Illuminated by the soft light of the lamps, two magnificent deerskin adornments lay before him–a man's beaded tunic with matching fringed trousers, and nestled beside that, a matching beaded fringed dress for his woman. Replacing the items he slowly closed the trunk and prepared for bed. Tomorrow would be its unveiling.

It was 5:00 a.m. when a scream from a cougar just outside the cabin door startled Dan from his sleep. Running, with pistol in hand, he flung open the door. In full view of the beam of his flashlight, a large cougar crouched with its ears laid back flat against its bleeding head, poised for attack and staring up into the dark, empty night sky.

"The eagles! Damn, that dumbass cougar looking for an easy nighttime meal, sure picked the wrong tree this time," he chuckled.

Standing on a limb thirty feet above in the beam of his light was the female eagle, wings arched, preparing for a second attack should this unwelcome intruder dare to scale her tree again. Above Dan's head came a whoosh as the male eagle swooped in for one last attempt at scalping this cowering cat with his massive, razor sharp talons fully extended.

Boom, Boom. The silence of the forest shattered as two flashes of fire burst from the barrel of Dan's gun, the bullets pinging the ground in the blackness, right behind the big cat's tail. Leaping into the air, seemingly being attacked from all directions, the big cat decided it was time for an immediate retreat. Lunging as far off into the blackness as he could, he raced out of both Dan's and the swooping eagle's range.

Amused by the situation, Dan broke out into a loud laugh. He had never seen this local cougar he called Spooky flee for his life. It had always been the other way around with some other poor creature running for theirs.

"You'd better stay the hell out of here, Spooky!" Dan yelled. "I'm going to have a lady friend here today, and if I see you again, my aim will be right on target!"

Chapter 6

At exactly 9:00 a.m. Dan was about to place a firm knock on Hanna's door when suddenly it opened.

"Morning, Daniel. I've been up since dawn. I'm just so excited. I thought you may have changed your mind after yesterday."

"Not on your life, pretty lady. Not in a million years!"

Stopping by a small diner in town for a quick breakfast before heading out, the two of them talked about the day they had first met. It had been a morning just like this one, and Dan was just as nervous now as he had been the first time he saw her. Hanna had seen these facial twitches before and giggled.

"Mr. Rawlins, don't tell me you're going to get all bashful and run out on me again. The last time I saw you this nervous, you were running out of the White Bird Diner and you didn't come back for two weeks."

"After all the bragging I've done, I just hope you like the place, that's all. I just want you to love it as much as I do."

"Whatever you've done, Daniel, I am sure I'll love it. Now, cowboy, what say we saddle up in that truck of yours and go see that cabin. With all that time you've been keeping me away from it, I was beginning to think you were seeing another girl."

When they arrived at the cabin, Dan walked Hanna up to the door, past clusters of wildflower blooms he had placed in the hollowed-out branches of pine that lined the cobblestone path. Slowly opening the door, Dan gave Hanna a deep bow, and with a sweeping motion of his arm, begged her entrance.

"Welcome to my humble home, Hanna. This is our place."

Wide eyed, Hanna stood in total silence. What she saw was the most beautiful place she could have ever imagined. She could almost reach out and touch the love and warmth that seemed to permeate the air.

From the lace adornments gracing the windows to the detailed furnishings he had made from nature itself, from the sprawling bearskin rug to the wall montage collected from all reaches, to the potbelly stove to keep them warm in winter, she stood in the center of a part of his life and heart.

"Well, go ahead and say it. I know it's not much...."

"Don't you *dare* ever say that again." Grasping Dan's cheeks, she looked up into his eyes and her lips melted into his.

"Daniel Rawlins, this is more than I could have ever imagined. This is not a cabin you have brought me to; this is a part of your life itself. Everywhere I look I see the things you've made, and I see they're filled with your love and tenderness."

"Now wait just a minute. Before you start to get all mushy on me, honey, there's a lot more I want you to see."

Having received her approval of the main room, Dan took Hanna's hand, and like an excited little boy, he led her to the kitchen where the nickel-trimmed cook stove stood.

"Now this is where you can cook, and over here is the bedroom. I can build on to it later if you want me to."

As Hanna entered the bedroom her eyes fell upon his most magnificent creation. Poised majestically to greet her was a massive four-poster bed built from the surrounding pines. Cascading from the four pillars, the laced-trimmed netting looked like a floating cloud. A beautiful double wedding ring-patterned quilt adorned the plush mattress.

While Hanna was temporarily transfixed by all of this beauty, she hadn't heard Dan tell her about how he had covered the plank floor with a mosaic carpet of furred deer hides to warm her bare feet, or that Mrs. Mears had given him the bed quilt the woman had quilted after he had told her about Hanna.

"My God, Daniel, this is the most beautiful bed I have ever seen!"

"Come on, Hanna. Let me show you the outside. There's something I want you to see."

Something he wanted her to see, she thought. What in the world could he show her that would in any way rival what he had already shown her?

Following Dan, tightly clasping his hand, he led her out the rear door of the cabin, down the four half-log steps and onto a path of small river rocks that gently sloped toward a gurgling sound hidden in the trees.

As she made her way between two massive pines, the path widened into a large cleared area surrounded by a sea of ferns. Wisps of steam rose into the coolness of the air from where the gentle gurgling beckoned. Standing on a gathering of large flat stones Dan had placed as if to build an alter to the Gods, Hanna looked down into a gently swirling pool of warm, bubbling water.

"How do you like it? We even have a bathtub."

"My goodness, Daniel. If you come up with just one more surprise for me today, I just think I'm gonna faint right here in front of you."

"Well, please don't faint, but I do have to ask you for a great big favor."

"Anything, Daniel. Anything at all."

Grasping both of Hanna's hands, Dan looked into her eyes and slowly lowered himself to his knees. Taking a deep breath as he felt the warmth of her hands, he cleared his throat. "Hanna, I know that we have only known each other for a short time, but what I have learned about you is all I need to know. For some unknown reason I walked into that cafe that morning, and it was as if someone had put you there for me to find.

"You don't know everything about my past, but *that* you can learn in time. I promise there are no demons residing in me to harm you, only a heart filled with love for how you make me feel. It's for that reason that I'm asking you to do me the greatest favor of my life. Miss Hanna Hunter, will you marry me?"

Stunned, Hanna's knees went weak. "Daniel Rawlins, I told you…Oh my God, Daniel. That's not a favor. My God, Daniel, *yes*!"

Dan leaped to his feet and embraced Hanna's quivering body and lips. As the two lover's hearts melded in this moment of passion, the mist rising from the warm pool encircled them. Like a halo of approval formed by the spirits of their ancestors, the mist suddenly increased in size, swirling up high into the sky, as an announcement to all, of a new birth in the circle of life.

Hearing the words he had desperately wanted to hear, Dan's nervousness faded away. There was so much more he wanted to show her: his eagles nesting in the tree in front of his cabin, the crevasse in the rock upstream that spawned the warm waters of the pool. He wanted her to know everything about this place, the place they would make their home for all their days to come.

For the next several hours they wandered over every inch of the property surrounding the cabin. Dan pointed out the tracks left by the fleeing cougar he called Spooky, and related the story of how those tracks had come to be there.

Dan and Hanna had never felt so much at peace in their lives. All of the wounds of their past youth that had lain dormant, festering silently inside them, suddenly had been healed. Now was not the time to languish any longer in the past. This was the time to make plans for their wedding ceremony that would seal their new life together for all eternity.

"I'll need to get something to wear. Dan, what is your favorite color? Do you think I should try to make a list of who we should invite? Who should we get to marry us, Daniel? I don't know very many people here–"

"Stop! Now look around you. Hanna, did you really think that with all I did to bait this trap for you, I didn't have a few other things you haven't seen yet, just in case you had told me yes? Let's just enjoy the rest of the afternoon together, and we can talk about all the other stuff before next Saturday, okay?"

"Next Saturday? What do you mean *next Saturday*? Now wait just a minute Daniel Rawlins. You mean to tell me that you already planned for our wedding to be held a week from now when you hadn't even asked me to marry you? Didn't you think I might have wanted to say just a few things about all of this? Didn't you–"

"Now wait just a minute, Mrs. Rawlins-to-be. I had no intention of planning anything except for something special for you if you had honored me by accepting my marriage proposal.

"The only thing we *do* have in common that can never change is our Indian heritage. We might want to consider some of the customs of our past, don't you think?"

"All right my little Indian princess, we need to head back before I scoop you up and show you just how wonderful that little bubbling hot springs of ours really feels. It wouldn't be right to cuddle under that double wedding ring quilt Mrs. Mears gave us before we actually made it legal, now, would it? But if you're game...."

"Daniel Rawlins, I'm sure I didn't just hear what I heard."

"Now, let's see. My favorite color is blue, the only friends I have I can count on one hand, and I don't need a haircut till next month. So see there? Other than you gathering up what stuff you have back at the motel and telling the manager you're moving out next Friday, there really isn't anything else you need to do. So let's go close up the cabin, little sweetie. I need to get you home. I have work to do."

Hanna just smiled. "I guess you're right, Big Chief. From the looks of things around your village here, I wouldn't want to upset you. Heck, if I started wanting to do some planning for our big pow-wow, you might decide to hold a sun dance ritual, pierce me, then sacrifice me by throwing me into that old boiling pot you have out back–like Fox and Coyote did to them old Seven Devils."

Smiling, having felt that she had bested him with all this talk of Indian rituals, Hanna pulled Dan close to her side and hugged him as they strolled together back to his truck. With all that this man had already done for her, she knew that whatever he had planned would be his crowning jewel toward their lifelong bond. She was going to trust him with her life; she could certainly trust him in his decisions.

As they made their way back into town, the events of the day replayed in Hanna's mind. With the flurry of events, she hadn't given any thought to the name he had called her when he had made his proposal. *Hanna Hunter?* She didn't remember ever telling Dan her last name. It wasn't that she wouldn't have; she just never recalled him asking, or that the subject ever came up during any of their previous conversations.

Hanna pushed the thought to the back of her mind. She had just been proposed to by the man she knew she loved. She must have told him; she probably just didn't remember. She certainly wasn't going to dampen the euphoric feeling of happiness she was feeling right now. Seven days from now she would be standing in front of a minister saying *"I do"* to her soul mate.

Dan and Hanna parted with one last kiss as he left her at the motel. Waving goodbye, she held her emotions back. She wanted to run back to his truck. She wanted to be with him now. She didn't understand why Dan hadn't asked her to stay with him.

Dan wanted more than anything to stay with Hanna that night, but his proposal had set certain things into motion that he had failed to consider. He was going to marry this woman, and he wanted their bond to be one of total honesty. He had taken an oath of silence, but now the contract he had made with the man in White Bird needed to be renegotiated. It had to be done now, regardless of the consequences. He headed north to White Bird.

Chapter 7

It was almost 10:00 that night before Dan returned to the cabin. Frustrated, still carrying the emotions of the day within him, he reached into the cabinet and broke the seal of a bottle of whiskey he had kept in the cabin just in case he might need it one day for relief of a rattlesnake bite or some such event. Although it was unlike him, he needed a stiff drink.

The meeting with the gentleman in White Bird had not gone the way he had hoped. Rick Mears got a call from Bob Grimsley who had set up Dan's employment in Riggins when he had first arrived. Grimsley had asked about a young girl Dan had been spending time with. It was when Dan had been invited for supper with Rick Mears and his wife that Dan had learned Hanna's last name, but he hadn't given it a thought until now.

When he had told Mrs. Mears that he'd made up his mind to propose to Hanna, Mrs. Mears had commented about how she thought the name *Hunter* wasn't only beautiful, but how appropriate it was that the orphanage had given the little Indian girl that name when she had arrived there.

How could Mrs. Mears have known Hanna's last name if her husband hadn't discussed it, and how did they learn of it? Dan's day-to-day existence had been so normal, he had forgotten just how different the new life he had agreed to really was going to be. His contact in White Bird, for some reason, had ordered Hanna's background to be investigated, and Dan now realized why. Up until now, Hanna had not been part of the loop of secrecy. She hadn't been vetted to assure she didn't have friends among any of the local militias.

It was midnight when the headlights of two vehicles pulled to the front of Dan's cabin. Grimsley, the man from White Bird, occupied the first. In the second vehicle rode Mears and another man Dan didn't know, named Bill Sands.

A long discussion took place that night in the cabin. Dan had violated a basic precept of his employment: Everything in his personal life, anything he did outside of his normal everyday activities, was to be reported, and he knew it. Dan's undisclosed relationship with Hanna had found its way to White Bird through Mears, not Dan. Dan, without thinking, had violated a cardinal rule. They would forgive him this time, but any further lapses in protocol wouldn't be tolerated.

Just before sunrise the men concluded their business and drove away, confident that their actions had been appropriate. The matter was closed. The names of those who had attended would never be revealed to anyone, and Dan's life would continue just as it had before Hanna Hunter had entered the picture.

Broadcast on the radio the following day, a news report circulated that Bill Sands would be replacing Deputy Rick Mears in Riggins. Deputy Mears was being promoted to the position of interim Sheriff for Idaho County, replacing Robert Grimsley who had announced his resignation. No explanation was ever given and would remain a mystery to Dan. He would chalk it up to the old adage, strictly on a need to know basis, and he obviously didn't fall into that category.

Chapter 8

Just after 7:00 a.m., Dan knocked on Hanna's door. She, too, had risen early, still whirling from the previous day. Opening the door, she saw Dan wearing a somber look on his face, and her heart sank. Had he changed his mind? Had she done something to give him second thoughts?

"Oh, Dan, is something wrong? Are you okay?"

"May I come in, Hanna? I think we should talk. I haven't been totally honest with you. There's something I need to tell you about that may change your mind about marrying me. I just want you to know everything but I can't...." Dan slowly closed the door behind him.

Almost two hours later, Dan opened the door again and turned to Hanna.

"I love you, Dan. I will always love you." Hanna assured him. "Now you go do whatever it is you do and leave me alone for a few days. I have a wedding to get ready for, silly boy! There are just some things a girl has to do to get ready, even if the groom is the one planning her wedding." Dan drew Hanna into his arms and kissed her.

"I love you, too, Hanna Hunter. You don't have to do a thing. You're beautiful just the way you are."

The next few days seemed to pass in a blur for both of them. From time to time Dan would drive by the motel, but he didn't stop. He had promised Hanna that he was going to take care of everything for the wedding, and by God he wasn't going to let her down, no matter what.

On Friday Dan left the small town of Lapwai, located just outside of Lewiston. He had made a trip there to pick up what he hoped would be a very special gift for Hanna. Also in Lapwai, he'd located a man named Long Bow, a Nez Perce spiritual leader. Long Bow was a descendant of Shmoqula who had been a Nez Perce warrior as well as a shaman. Dan asked Long Bow to officiate the wedding.

Stopping one last time, Dan arranged for Rick Mears and his wife to pick up Hanna and bring her to the cabin the next morning. He'd asked their guests to arrive at 11:00 a.m. and to be available for Hanna in case she needed help with anything. There would be no maid of honor, no wedding court–the wedding party would simply consist of Dan, Hanna, and the shaman, Long Bow.

Even though Dan and Hanna had been abandoned by their parents, the blood of the Nez Perce people still coursed through their veins. They had decided that their ancestors should play a part in their future.

Just after 9:00 a.m. the Mears arrived with Hanna in tow. Hanna and Dan wouldn't see each other before the ceremony.

Taking control of the situation, Mrs. Mears instructed her husband to get out of her way and go help Dan while she tended to Hanna.

Like a loving mother, Mrs. Mears guided Hanna into Dan's bedroom and closed the door. On top of the bed, Hanna found a woven basket filled with red rose petals, and a bundle wrapped in white linen. Inside the bundle was one of the most beautiful red-dyed, ankle-length, beaded deerskin dress Hanna had ever seen.

From the shed in the rear of the cabin two men and a young boy emerged quickly, then made their way through the overgrown arrow leaf on the hillside leading to the creek below. They were married men, but still, their nerves were a bit on edge for Dan's sake as they shared a touch of whiskey before the ceremony began.

Just before 11:00, Mr. and Mrs. Altman, the owners of the motel where Hanna had worked, along with a small group of other close friends, arrived. Dave Pettigrew who worked at the building supply in Riggins and had also helped Dan many times when he had worked on the cabin, gathered the guests off to the side of the cabin and waited for Long Bow's signal.

Suddenly out of the sky, two majestic eagles swooped down past the waiting attendees, then dramatically ascended into the treetops. Their keen eyes scanned the area as if to ask why these strangers had come to this mystical place in the forest. The two mighty birds then came to attention as the Indian, Long Bow, made his appearance below them.

It was time. Mrs. Mears emerged from the rear of the cabin and joined the other guests just as the sound of a drum filled the air from the direction of the spring.

A column of white smoke rose from behind Long Bow. The shaman was dressed in native Indian beaded deerskin from top to bottom and sported a spectacular eagle-feather headdress. He stood silently atop a boulder overlooking the steaming hot spring.

The hot springs pool greeted the guests as they approached the creek. Pettigrew divided their number into two columns to form a pathway for Hanna, which led up to a bridge of thick planking that had been laid across the pool. On the other side of the pool, standing on a massive flat slab of granite, stood Daniel Rawlins.

Outfitted with a beaded deerskin tunic that cascaded down to his fringed matching trousers and beaded moccasins, he stood silently as Long Bow outstretched his arms and began a solemn chant to the gods in his native Nez Perce *Sahaptin* language.

A broad smile appeared on Dan's face as his precious Migisi appeared from behind the pines, cradling a small hand-woven basket. Her moccasined feet carried her silently down the stone path and across the plank bridge to the large alter stone. There she turned, looked silently into Dan's eyes, and returned his smile.

As they stood in silence, Long Bow ended his chant and turned his palms toward the sky, looking down on the couple below him.

Taking one small step forward, Hanna extended the basket toward Dan. "Daniel Rawlins, I give to you this basket of rose petals as a gift from my heart. I give you my promise to always love you and comfort you, to be yours and yours alone, for all of eternity.

Then Dan, producing a single white eagle feather from beneath his tunic, the special gift he had gotten in Lapwai, responded.

"Hanna Migisi Hunter, to you I give this feather that represents my undying love for you. I promise to watch over you as the great eagles watch over us all. To forever protect and care for you and to be yours and yours alone for all of eternity."

Long Bow slowly turned and faced the rising column of smoke behind him. Retrieving a handful of powder from a leather pouch, he cast the powder into the smoke and a large ball of flame suddenly rose skyward as the drumbeats again began to sound.

The ceremony ended. Daniel Rawlins and Hanna Hunter were now Mr. and Mrs. Daniel Rawlins, man and wife by the customs of the Nez Perce Nation.

The guests began to applaud as the couple kissed, then turned to smile at those who had just witnessed the joining of their two souls. As Dan and Hanna left the altar and passed by their admirers, the men called out, "Way to go Dan!" "Congratulations, War Eagle!" "Thought the old Chief was going to boil you in the spring, Dan boy!" making Dan and Hanna chuckle.

The female guests, however, just shook their heads at the men in disgust. How could they make jokes after witnessing such a moving ceremony?

Not about to engage in such irreverent behavior, the ladies quickly stepped forward to surround Hanna like a group of mama does defending their vulnerable fawn.

Hanna's defenders drowned out the men's comments by showering Hanna with "How wonderful that you chose a traditional Indian ceremony" and "How you just look like the most beautiful, sweet, radiant little Indian princess we've ever seen."

"I'm ready for the hoedown!" one of the men shouted.

"Okay," Dan piped up. "There's food and drink for everyone, but I need you fellas to give me a hand with that table over there in the shed. God forbid, I ain't lettin' you guys mess up all the hard work I did inside for Hanna." When the laughter died down, Dan got serious. "We both can't thank you all enough for being here with us today. You will never know how much it means that you, our adopted family, have been a part of this very special ceremony. Thank you!"

Deputy Mears shot the cork from a magnum of champagne as Dave Pettigrew drew his bow across his fiddle, filling the trees with the sounds of celebration. Hanna and Dan reveled in what both of them had always sought–true love and affection from those they would always hold dear.

Although Long Bow would have preferred a more traditional Indian dance instead of the impromptu square dance breaking out in front of him, he stripped off his ceremonial headdress, gave a silent nod toward the couple, and quickly joined in the dance.

As the afternoon shadows fell upon the gathering, the group, one by one, said their congratulatory farewells, leaving Hanna and Dan to begin their new life together. As the last vehicle disappeared from sight, Dan turned to Hanna and smiled.

"Whatever life brings us, wherever our travels lead us, whatever fate God will choose for us, I want you to know that I will always love you and be with you forever."

As their lips met, their two hearts pounded out a rhythm of desire. Their love lit a fire of passion between them that few would ever know. During the ceremony, they had become not just husband and wife, but a man and a woman transformed into one being.

Inside the cabin, Dan prepared a warming fire, then illuminated the interior with a smattering of candles while Hanna adorned herself with a transparent white nightgown Mrs. Mears had given her for her wedding night. Hearing a faint click from the opening bedroom door, Dan turned to find himself looking upon the most beautiful creature he had ever seen. "Hanna, you look just like an angel."

"Daniel, if you would like to change now, I would like you to escort me to the pool at the spring. I believe you said it is a wonderful place to bathe. Now go hurry up, my love. You wouldn't want me to go down there alone and have that old cougar Spooky devour me for dinner, would you?"

For the next week, Dan and Hanna holed up in the cabin like two bandits hiding from the law. With the exception of the one and only trip Dan made into Riggins for supplies, Dan was never more than an arm's reach from his bride as they blended their two lives together.

Summer had come in full swing, and heat permeated the Salmon River canyon.

When their first week together came to an end, Dan had to go back to work. He had chores to do not only at the cabin but down by the river where he maintained two acres of land near Big Salmon Road. He held a lease from the Forest Service for the property where he would build a small pole barn and stalls to house three pack mules he had purchased for his hunting guide service that would start that coming fall.

Completing his work, with Hanna proudly looking on, Dan struck a final blow with his hammer, securing the hand-carved sign reading "Rawlins Pack Service," to a cross timber above the gate leading to the pole barn. Hanging by chains under the banner sign was a second sign that read "Hunting / Fishing Guided Trips." and a telephone number.

Dan had hired an answering service to gather possible client names and phone numbers. He would then return the clients' calls. Clients never would contact Dan directly.

The weeks passed quickly, and in Hells Canyon the stifling summer heat soon gave way to the cool Pacific breezes that were now pushing billowing cumulous clouds from the coast into Idaho. On the 24th of August, Dan got a call from an old Army buddy who had been coming to the Hells Canyon area with his father to hunt since he was a boy.

"Is this the same Dan Rawlins that used to be with the 101st?" the man on the other end of the line asked.

"It might be. Do I know you?" Dan cautiously responded.

"It's Jimmy Hill. If this is the same Dan Rawlins, you bet your ass you know me. Airborne All The Way, Sir."

Yes, Dan knew him. He had been in training with Jim Hill at Fort Benning Georgia's Sniper School before they had both been deployed to Vietnam with the 101st Airborne Division.

"Yep, this is the same Dan Rawlins, Jimmy. How in the world did you get my number? I sure didn't think I would ever hear from you again."

"Well, Dan, old friend, my dad passed away a few years back, and when it comes to hunting season, you know me. Anyway, he used to bring me up here as a kid to hunt elk. I just blew into Riggins, and when I asked around if anyone knew of a good guide that wasn't already booked, a guy suggested that maybe they would know at the sheriff's office. A deputy there gave me your number. Small world, ain't it, Dan? Who would of thought?"

After a brief conversation with Hill, Dan agreed to meet with him in town to discuss a proposed hunt. Hill may have been a former army acquaintance, but he was far from what Dan would call a good friend. The last time he had spoken to Hill was when they had gotten their orders after graduation at Fort Benning. The last thing he remembered Hill talking about was how he was now a licensed professional VC killer that couldn't wait until he got the chance to dance with some "rice-eating whore," and blow someone's head off.

Hill certainly wasn't someone Dan was going to invite to his home, but since most of the really hardcore deer and elk hunters had already made arrangements for guided hunting trips months or even a year in advance, Dan thought that this might be a good opportunity to get his name out, and even possibly meet other future clients as they mingled around town waiting to head out on their hunts.

After meeting with Hill, and having received no other inquiries for his services during the scheduled upcoming hunting season, Dan agreed to take him into the mountains.

Hill had told Dan that he had two other men who would be flying into Boise in three days, but in the meantime wanted to do some fishing prior to the opening of elk season. Hill and his friends wanted to hunt in an area down in the Sawtooth Wilderness area near the Queens River, and that left little time for Dan to make his final arrangements.

Dan gave Hill a few tips on where he could do some fishing near Riggins while he waited for his friends to arrive. Dan would need to hustle to gather together gear and supplies for the group that had planned to spend ten days at Sawtooth. Dan instructed Hill, who would be picking up his friends, to meet him at the Queens River Trailhead off Highway 21 in three days. Dan would be providing three mules to pack in their gear, and saddle horses for the trip.

With the help of a rancher friend, four saddle horses and the fully packed mules would be standing ready when the group arrived. They would head into the wilderness area at Queens River trailhead and proceed to the Black Warrior Trail up into the mountains where Dan would leave the group to hunt. On the ninth day out, Dan would return with the mules and mounts, bringing the hunters and their game back to the trailhead.

The group had only been on the trail for maybe an hour or so when the sound of a gunshot and breaking glass made the hair on Dan's neck bristle. Yanking his horse's reins, he whirled around just in time to catch one of his charges cock the hammer of a pistol, point it toward a trail marker, and shoot. Furious, Dan spurred his mount and headed straight for the man.

"If I see one more jackass stunt like that, this trip ends here and now!"

If his ears could have smoked, Dan's would have been belching steam like the boiler of a coal-fired locomotive fighting its way up a steep mountain grade. Gritting his teeth to hold back the ass chewing of a lifetime he wanted to lavish upon this idiot, he turned his horse and rode up to where Hill's horse stood.

"You handle this, Jimmy. You tell that whiskey-drinking idiot friend of yours he's a guest in my forest. This ain't some San Francisco dump where he can just leave his shit and shoot up the place. Either you make it clear to your group how to act like responsible people, or this trip is over."

Other than the sound of a rider clearing his throat or an occasional whinny of one of the animals, nobody spoke much on the remainder of the trip to their selected campsite on the Black Warrior Trail.

That afternoon Dan found a place along a stream where the men made quick work of catching an evening meal of brook and rainbow trout. The men exchanged pleasantries, and nothing more was said of the earlier incident, nor was it ever repeated.

Ten days later it was time to leave. As planned, Dan had arrived with the mounts the afternoon before. Leaving the men to hunt, he had corralled the animals about a mile from the trailhead and had driven back to Riggins to spend a few days with Hanna. Now it was time to get these yahoos off the mountain and out of the canyon.

At the edge of the camp hung the carcass of a small bull elk that one man in the group had harvested the day before. Although Dan had formed an opinion early on about the inexperience of these big-game hunters, at least someone in the group, whom he assumed had been Jim Hill, had the presence of mind to let the animal bleed out in the cool night air.

With the game packed in coolers and an embarrassing small rack of horns trussed to the ass of an ass, Dan wasted little time mounting up and escorting Hill and the other two questionable characters, back to their vehicle and out of his life.

As the men transferred their belongings into Jim's Land Rover, Jim took Dan off to the side and thanked him for his patience and apologized for his friends' behavior.

"Here ya go, Dan. Thirty-five crisp Ben Franklins for ya. I'll give ya a call about this time next year and we'll do this again."

"Well, Jim, I was hoping I wasn't gonna have to say this, but unfortunately, I think this is going to be my last trip for quite some time. I sure would have liked to have done this with you all again real soon but unfortunately, me and the missus are moving up to Canada in the spring. It was sure great to see you again, old buddy. Now you take care."

With that, the men parted company and Dan never saw Jimmy Hill again.

Chapter 9

Jimmy Hill's group would be the last Dan would take out that season. Dan hadn't really expected to do much guiding his first year. The only inquiries he had gotten since Hill had been there were some passers-by who'd just wanted information. What they really wanted was free advice about where they could kill a world-record Boone & Crocket trophy buck or elk. Clearly, they had no intention of putting up the money for a guide.

That suited Dan and Hanna just fine. With the money Dan had made from Jimmy Hill, and with the income from doing some odd jobs around Riggins, he always seemed to have money in his pockets to get them what they needed.

Dan had gone out on two occasions to look for overdue hunters, one over in Hells Canyon, and the second one up near the town of Moscow. He had assisted the Sheriff's Department in retrieving the bodies of two flatlanders who had underestimated Idaho's avalanche dangers.

It seemed that two idiots from the city had thought it would be a good idea to drive through a mountain pass in a jeep in heavy snow, and then honk a hand-held air horn to listen for its echo off the canyon walls.

Six days later when the weather cleared, a forestry helicopter spotted the red top of what was left of their mangled jeep in a snow-filled ravine. Dan and his mule assisted in pulling what was left of their partially scavenged bodies to a road where they could be loaded for the remainder of their ride to the coroner. Nothing was listed about the men being intoxicated or for them possessing two ounces of marijuana later found in their jeep. Mother Nature had already held court and had issued a death sentence as punishment for their folly.

When early spring arrived, Dan got a call from the newly elected sheriff of Idaho County, Rick Mears.

"Morning, Dan. How is my girl Hanna? You two been hibernating all winter in that cozy cabin of yours?"

After a few rounds of pleasantries, the conversation quickly turned to business. Mears inquired about how Dan was getting along with Mears' replacement, Deputy Sands, in Riggins.

Although Dan had had some dealings with Bill Sands over the winter, they hadn't spent much time getting to know each other that well.

"Well, Dan, I'll let you go. Tell Hanna that me and the missus said hello. If you two ever get tired of playing footsy and get up here to Grangeville, we would both love to see you."

By now Dan and Hanna had become true members of the community. Hanna had taken a part-time job as a teaching assistant at the elementary school in town, and Dan was now considered one of the best hunting and fishing guides in the northern part of the state.

In the fall of their second year, Dan returned from a week-long trip where he had taken some hunters to a camp near LoLo Pass, close to the eastern border of Idaho. As he walked into the cabin, Hanna was standing in the middle of the room dressed in her sheer white nightgown. It was two o'clock in the afternoon.

"Well, you old sweaty cowboy, it took longer than I had expected, but guess what, handsome. I'm late, and it's all your fault! Now what do you have to say for yourself?"

"You mean you're... you mean I'm... you mean I'm gonna be a daddy?"

Grinning from ear to ear, Hanna replied, "You bet your silver spurs you are, Daniel. I just found out at the clinic yesterday afternoon that I'm six weeks along. We're going to have us a little Rawlins."

"Clear my calendar, Mrs. Rawlins. You're going to need some direct supervision for a while. No more trail riding for me for the next few months. You're going to get my undivided attention."

Throughout the winter and into the spring, Dan remained at Hanna's beck and call. On more than one occasion Hanna threatened to run off with another man–one who didn't even like her–if Dan didn't stop being such a pest. "Sit down I'll get that, honey." "You shouldn't be doing that." "I'll cook dinner, dear." "You shouldn't have to..." He was a mess, and Hanna couldn't wait for the baby to arrive.

Dan was fast asleep when he felt Hanna's warm breath on his eyelids. "Daniel, you better get dressed, sweetheart. It's time."

"It's time!" he blurted, almost falling headlong into the door. Hanna stepped to the side like a matador clearing the path for a charging bull.

"Yes, dear. I think we need to go into town right now. Daniel, my water broke. Now put your pants on, honey. You're going to look mighty silly driving into town in your underwear. We wouldn't want our baby to think its daddy is a nut, now, would we?"

Nine frightful hours later, a young nurse came for Dan. He had just completed his sixth cigar after handing out eighteen others to passing strangers.

"Daniel Rawlins? Mr. Rawlins, Mrs. Rawlins and your daughter Maggie wanted me to ask you if you would like to meet them in their room."

Dan's knees suddenly turned to jelly. As his face began to turn an ashen gray and his sagging body headed straight for disaster, a grinning hospital attendant who happened to have a great deal of maternity waiting-room experience and the great Houdini's sleight of hand, quickly slid a wheelchair under Dan's rear, just as Dan was about to collide with the concrete floor.

With a snap of a vial of smelling salts, Dan regained his senses. Rising from the chair he held out a bouquet of flowers, the fast-thinking attendant had planted in his nervous fist.

"Mr. Rawlins," the attendant announced. May I have the pleasure of introducing you and the rest of the world to your daughter Maggie, six pounds four ounces, who brought nothing into this world with her but love."

Hanna reached out to Dan, their pink-faced newborn cradled snugly in her hands. "This is your daddy, Maggie. This is the man who created you. His name is Daniel."

After all of these years, Dan and Hanna had finally become whole. Now these two people who had never known *family* were immersed in it. They were now taking their first steps toward building a family tree, a tree that would grow for generations to come, a Rawlins Tree that the two of them would never allow to be destroyed.

Now that Maggie was part of their lives, Dan had to refocus. He needed to provide not only for his family but to fulfill obligations he had made in the past. He had a home, a wife, and now a new daughter, but he also had a job to be performed. This was now the time for him to market the skill he knew best–hunting.

During the winter months he had made several day trips into the mountains to scout the feeding patterns of the wildlife, as well as suitable terrain for camp locations for the upcoming fall hunts. Though his knowledge of the area had already been praised by others, Dan made it a priority to always keep a low profile when the conversations with the locals began to center around just where and when Dan did his scouting.

The day before Dan's 27th birthday, a man tapped him on the shoulder in Murdock's Feed & Grain.

"It's been awhile. We have a mutual friend that needs to talk to you, Daniel."

Dan didn't have to turn to look. The voice was one he remembered very well, the voice of his old sniper instructor, Master Sergeant William Goldsmith, U.S. Army, Retired.

"No, I can get it just fine," Dan responded, never turning to look at the man behind him.

"They keep most of the feed corn in the building out back. Just ask the guy at the counter. He can show you."

"Tonight at Sands' office. Ten o'clock. Come in the back," Goldsmith said as he turned and walked away.

Dan's knees locked. He never turned to look, but from the corner of his eye he could see the outline of a large figure disappear into the shadows of the storage barn.

When Dan returned home, Hanna met him at the door with a wide smile, holding Maggie in her arms, but he didn't respond with his normal outstretched arms. His eyes looked empty as he stared past her, and he entered the cabin as if she wasn't there.

"Dan, is there something wrong? Are you okay sweetheart? Talk to me Daniel. Is everything okay?"

"We have to talk, Hanna. I'm fine, but I just need a few minutes to gather my thoughts, that's all. I met a man in town today that I used to know. Remember what I told you before we got married? About how sometimes I have to do things that we just can't talk about together? Things I can never tell you about?"

"Yes, I remember. You mean about when you were–"

Dan stopped her. "I mean exactly that. Things I never want to be discussed again, not even now. There are things I can never tell you about my work and you just shouldn't ask. If you do, it could be very dangerous for both of us. It could even be dangerous for Maggie."

"I understand," Hanna said. "You just looked upset about something, is all."

"There's nothing wrong. It's just that some unexpected business has come up, and I have a meeting in town late this evening with a client. It may run very late."

"Maggie made a sound today that sounded like, *'Daddy'* I was just excited to tell you. You go get cleaned up. I made a stew for us. I think you're really going to like it. It's made out of everything you like...."

Hanna's words trailed off as Dan walked out the rear of the cabin, heading for the creek.

Little was said during dinner. Several times when Hanna tried to engage him in small talk, Dan retorted with sharp responses almost bordering on anger. That was certainly not like him. Hanna had seen Dan upset before, but he usually covered his dismay with a smile or a passing comment about how stupid he had been to have caused whatever the issue was in the first place.

"Hanna, I'm very sorry for the way I acted toward you this evening," Dan apologized. A lot of things have been on my mind that I wish I could talk about, but I can't. Just understand that I love you and that you don't need to worry about anything. This has nothing to do with anything but business."

For the next few hours Dan paced nervously around the cabin, even ignoring Hanna as she cradled the nursing Maggie. Hanna knew something very strange appeared to be troubling Dan, but as she had promised, she would not press him for information when he'd asked her not to do so.

"Daniel, I almost forgot. The eagles out front are getting ready to have babies, I think. When I was walking down to the stream this afternoon, I saw them together in the air. You know how they do with their feet kind of locked together? I think they were mating, don't you? I think they knew I was watching. Isn't it wonderful?"

"Hmm. I'd better go sweetheart. It's almost nine o'clock and I can't be late. Lock up, okay? I might be home pretty late so don't wait up for me. And don't go roaming around outside after I leave. I saw that damned cougar on the hill above the spring before dinner. I'm probably going to have to kill that son of a bitch if he keeps hanging that close. Its just not safe for the baby." Kissing both her and Maggie gently on their foreheads, Dan told them both that he loved them, then turned and disappeared through the rear cabin door into the night.

The front of the sheriff's station was dark when Dan arrived, but as he pulled around to the back, a yellow glow from a curtained window cast a backdrop of two silhouettes. One of the figures jabbed the other silhouette, then turned and disappeared from view as if a heated exchange had taken place and one had heard enough. Dan parked and entered through the back door.

"Well, there he is, the man of the hour."

Before this man could finish, Dan lashed out, "Shut up and cover the window. What in the hell do you think this is, a game? I live in this town. Don't you think those people at the store wonder who in the hell this stranger is just walking in off of the street looking for shit like –"

"Hey, the both of you just settle down. Dan, relax," a voice from the shadows interjected.

"Yeah, settle down. Dan is right. Cover the window." From the back of the room, out of the shadows stepped another familiar figure. "It's good to see you again, Dan." Bob Grimsley said, moving farther into the light. "You look surprised. You didn't think you were going to get rid of me that easily, did you? How is Hanna and the–"

"Look, let's get to the point!" Goldsmith cut him off. "The company has spent a considerable amount of its assets getting you set up here, Dan. We all have given you a great deal of leeway with this marriage, and we've let you do most anything you wanted up till now. The company thinks it's time to move forward and garner some return on its investment."

As Goldsmith began exerting his obvious senior position of authority, Grimsley and the others present in the room fidgeted nervously. Keeping to the shadows, not wanting to be singled out by disrupting him, Dan was the only one in the old drill sergeants' sights and that is the way the others wanted to keep it.

"By the way, Jimmy Hill sends his regards. If it hadn't been for that slap down you gave those two shoot-em-up mob guys you took hunting up to Sawtooth, he probably would never have gotten the inside connection he needed back in San Francisco.

"You didn't know it, but your ass chewing, along with Hill's Broadway act after you dumped them off, convinced those two bosses he was for real. They took that trip for the sole purpose of sizing Jimmy up. Hill needed you for his cover story, to get those guys to feel comfortable with him, and you closed the deal.

"A reunion of two old Army buddies, my ass." Goldsmith continued. "Damn, you played your part better than Jimmy ever expected. And hell, you didn't even know you were a player. Jimmy is in so tight now with those bastards, you would think he grew up with those two boys. They are laying out their whole operation to him.

"So now you know Jimmy works for us as well. Dan, old boy, the company didn't just set you up out here in the middle of nowhere to shovel mule shit, so let's get down to business. Sands over there has already been briefed. He will be your contact with the company. I have dossiers here on two men who are rumored to be heading up a new militia group up in the Bitterroot Range. One of the reported organizers, Samuel Crow, lives in Lowell. The second one, a guy by the name of Wilburton, is supposed to be holed up in the town of Orofino.

"So far, all we know is that they're calling themselves the Scott Peak Watchmen. An informant we turned over in Missoula told us that last fall, just before a snow storm, he got paid five hundred dollars to deliver a shipment to this group.

"He said he was told to bring a crate over from Missoula and deliver it to their contact at a campground at a place called Hoodoo Lake. The no-good son of a bitch said that he didn't know who set up the deal, just that he got his instructions in an envelope with the cash. The Missoula office is running that down, but anyway, that's not your concern.

"According to this guy, two men met him at the campground and opened this crate packed with 150 pounds of good old government C-4 plastic explosives. He said that the two men mentioned something about stashing the stuff in a cave over the winter, and that the one named Big G kept studying a topographical map of the area. There was a red circle on the map around a place called Elk Summit, and he heard one of them say, 'This stuff will damn sure show those federal boys we're serious!'

"It seems that our informant was on the run at the time and was facing somewhere around forty-five years for drug smuggling up into Canada when Border Patrol picked him up. Now he wants to flip and work off his beef with the U.S. Attorney's office.

"After doing a little more background checking on this asshole, we found out he has a cousin who is trained as a Combat Engineer with a National Guard unit over in Helena, Montana. The unit he is assigned to is missing 150 pounds of C-4. I think you get the picture. We think this guy is very credible.

"We also got a report from a sheriff up near Thompson Falls in Sanders County, Montana. The report said that a couple of prospectors working a small mine got their powder magazine broken into two weeks after the Guard unit had reported the C-4 missing.

"The only things that were taken from the miners was a spool of detonation cord, a 400- foot roll of time fuse, and 100 fuse blasting caps. A state trooper checked a vehicle with Idaho license plates registered to Garvin Wilburton at a campground two miles from that mine the night it was burglarized.

"The Deputy who took the burglary report just happened to pick up an empty Old Crow whiskey bottle at the scene that the miners didn't recognize and hadn't seen before. When they ran it through latent prints, bingo, they got two hits!

"The first print belonged to a Garvin Wayne Wilburton. You have his package. The second set of prints matched our other boy,

Samuel Little Feather Crow, whose last known address was up in Lowell.

"Our boy Wilburton got arrested in Thompson Falls for a bar fight, but gave the cops a bullshit address. When they went to pick him up on a warrant, the house address he gave was abandoned, and now he's nowhere to be found. It seems that our snitch also had another old friend whose name came up during his drug investigation. It just happens that our snitch got arrested for marijuana possession a few years back, and the guy in the truck with him was none other than Sam Crow who was living in Lowell.

"One of the names our informant gave us for one of the guys he met at the delivery site was Big G. We suspect that would be Wilburton. He said the other guy was an Indian around five foot six and skinny. That matches our boy Crow.

"These are two very bad boys Dan, and the company has given the green light on the both of them. We need you to do what needs to be done and make this whole thing go away. When you find the stash, just give the coordinates to Sands when you get back and we will send a team out to recover it. You just take care of the two gentlemen.

"Now, for our timeframe, this is the fourteenth. One of our people who has been keeping an eye on Crow said he overheard him talking to another man at a bar last week. Crow had said he was moving to Orofino at the end of the month. He told the guy he was going to help a buddy move some stuff up near Elk Ridge to a hunting camp they had in the Wilderness Area. We think that the thirtieth or the thirty-first is when they are going to move the stuff.

"We want you to be up at White Bird on the twenty-ninth. One of our choppers will airlift you and your supplies up to the fire lookout at Elk Peak Summit. They'll return for a pick up on the second. That should give you plenty of time to set up, do what you have to do, and get back for extraction. If you're not back at the summit by the second, you'll have to find your own way home.

Goldsmith stood and stretched, barely suppressing a yawn. "Now to finish up, Dan, we want you to take a few days and go camping with the little woman. We have a couple of guys that we're bringing in from the company to do a few modifications to your place. They will be here three days from now, and they'll need some privacy.

"You have that shed out back that will work nicely. Your cover will be that you're going to be one of Sands' reserve deputies – you know, for when he needs help looking for lost hunters and such. You're going to need a radio and maybe a few other things at the cabin, so the reserve deputy thing should take care of any suspicions if anyone asks.

"Now, to wrap things up, you have these two guy's photos. Commit them to memory and then destroy them. You can stash the other info away in case you need to review details before you head out.

"As soon as you complete your preparations for this, destroy all the information I'm giving you. Dan, these two men have to be stopped and stopped now. We're going to leave it up to you to coordinate this operation from the field. You're the one who will have 'eyes on' when they go to the stash.

"We will close the road from Highway 12 to Hoodoo Lake as soon as we get eyes on either of these guys. We closed the campground already, so the only people you should encounter in the canyon should be the targets.

"All right, I think we've covered just about everything. This meeting, which never took place, is now concluded. By the way, Dan, here's a package for you that you can keep when you've finished your work with these guys. It might come in handy on one of those Elk hunts of yours. I know you always appreciated the work the shop at Quantico did on those Remington's. I also packed you a Ghillie suit just for old times' sake. Now you be careful out there, boy. Sure would hate to lose you."

Chapter 10

Dawn was just about to break when Dan returned to the cabin. He could see a spattering of sparks rising from the stovepipe, evidence that Hanna was awake and stirring embers in the potbelly.

She met him at the door with a wide smile. "Nice to see you finally decided to come home, Mr. Rawlins. Have a nice time on the town with the boys? You must be exhausted. Maggie is still asleep if you would like to come and crawl into bed and cuddle with the two of us."

The last thing Dan remembered was feeling Hanna's warm body pressing against him and the touch of Maggie's soft little hand cradled in his big tough-skinned paw before he drifted off into a deep slumber.

It was almost two o'clock in the afternoon when Maggie's cries woke him.

"Sounds like somebody's hungry, Mommy. Nothing like a good two-legged alarm clock to wake up a malingering cowboy to remind him it's time to go to work."

"Did everything go well last night, or am I not allowed to ask, Daniel?"

"Everything went just fine, and yes, you can at least ask that. Tell you what, Hanna, the weather looks like it's going to be pretty nice for the next week. What say we pack a few things and take Maggie out for her first campout?

"I talked to Jim in town, and he wants to know if I could go up to the He Devils trailhead and check it out before the spring hiking crowd arrives. The forest service copter pilot called him and told him that he'd spotted an area from the air where the trail looked damaged. He said that a few good avalanche slides rocked the east slope about a month ago, and one of them looked like it might have taken out one of the main trails.

When Hanna didn't respond right away, Dan pressed, "It would be a good opportunity to exercise the mules, and we could spend a few days up at Mirror Lake. I could show Maggie what a great fishing guide her pa is. I think it would be fun for the three of us to get out and stretch our legs."

"It's still pretty early, don't you think?" Hanna asked, concerned. "Would it be safe to take Maggie up there and camp in the cold?"

"Hanna, my dear, you said you were a descendent of the great Chief White Bird, and I, of course, probably descended from the great Chief Joseph, or at the very least one of his long-lost cousins. So if you blend both of our DNA together, little Maggie possesses the same Nez Perce genes her ancestors did. They didn't have any problems camping out, did they?"

Again, Hanna seemed reluctant. "It'll be great. This time of year the mountains will be beautiful. Jim said that the snow melt around Mirror Lake is almost complete, so that won't be a problem. You know how you like to watch the eagles. This time of year they should be going crazy getting their nests ready. Come on,

Hanna. Let's do it. We'll have a great time just by ourselves before all the tourists show up and spoil our privacy.

"We can leave the day after tomorrow, I'll run into town for some supplies and get the tack for the mules ready. I'll take three of them up to Windy Gap first thing in the morning so they can shake out there winter cobwebs, and then, away we go."

Dan finally convinced Hanna that it would be safe for Maggie, so Hanna began to get excited. Scouring the cabin for anything she could think of that they may need, she was just about to finish up when Dan returned, sporting his favorite sweat-stained cowboy hat, his rifle, encased in buckskin, resting on his shoulder.

"Well, now, if you don't look like a picture right out of a Hollywood western, Mr. Rawlins, big gun and all. I think the only thing you're missing is a pair of sheepskin chaps and a jingling pair of muleskinner spurs strapped to those filthy old bull skin boots of yours. My goodness, Dan Rawlins, you sure know how to make a young woman feel safe, but if you don't get those boots of yours with all that mule crap caked on them out of my living room right this second, you're going to need more than that rifle to protect yourself."

Dan grinned over Hanna's praise of his outfit, but her admonishment over his filthy boots may have been a bit overstated. He had forgotten her golden rule: act like a cowboy if you want, but, *no boots in the house!*"

It was a beautiful morning as the three of them made their way up Seven Devils Road to Windy Gap. It was only 10 a.m. and the temperature had already reached almost 70 degrees when they mounted the mules and headed down the same trail Dan had taken her on when they had first met.

"My God, Daniel, just look at it. It's just so beautiful. Look over there, Maggie. Your daddy is going to show you some big bad Devils. Won't that just be so exciting for his little angel?"

"I hope she grows up to love it as much as I do, Hanna," Dan said. "Whoever would have thought anything this majestic could have once been so violent? Every time I come here it always amazes me. Its vastness and beauty, Hanna, have you ever seen anything so beautiful?"

"Well, as a matter of fact, Daniel, I believe I have, and her name is Maggie. Now be quiet and watch where that mule of yours is leading us. We can look at all these magnificent surroundings when we get to a wide, flat spot, someplace other than the side of this cliff you have us walking down.

"We need to stop up ahead, Dan. I need to change Maggie, and I could stand to stretch my legs, okay?" My backside isn't quite broke in yet for the back of this mule."

Dan had never seen the canyon so lovely? Everywhere, spring grasses unfurled, now released from the bonds of the winter blanket of snow. Where the sun had given warmth to the soil, four o'clocks covered the hillsides and meadows. Douglas fir and Ponderosa pine reached high into the sky, watched over by the sporadic stands of Engelmann spruce atop the ridgeline.

The sub-alpine terrain provided a backdrop for a small herd of mountain bighorn sheep.

"Hanna, look over there. Aren't they spectacular?"

Looming up from the canyon floor stood the surrounding peaks of the Devils in all their glory.

"Okay, Migisi. See if you can remember. What are these monsters' names?"

"Let me see now. Those two are He and She. The top of that one over there is Goblin. Then there is Ogre, Twin Imps, Tower of Babel and the last is Devils Throne.

"Very good, sweetheart, I think I'll claim He Devil, you can have She Devil, Maggie can have the Ogre and that will leave the other four peaks for our other children to lay claim to. How does that sound to you?"

"Daniel Rawlins, if you think I'm going to spend the rest of my life having babies so you can give away mountains, you have another thought coming. I'm not saying Maggie can't have a brother or sister maybe, but me, you, and five other little Rawlins in that cabin would be just a little too much, don't you think?

Dan turned to her with a wide smile. "Get up, mule... yup mule... easy mule."

The rest of the trail ride to Mirror Lake was filled with great joy as the three of them took in the beauty of their surroundings. With the exception of Dan's occasional interjections about being careful and mindful of the possible dangers, it was a wonderful journey for Hanna.

"Remember, Hanna, we have to keep a sharp eye out. You know there are black bear, cougar, and wolves around this area. We might even encounter a charging big horn sheep ram. I don't think we'll have any problems with rattlesnakes or poison ivy this early with the snow and all, but there have been rumored sightings of grizzly bears stirring and roaming the canyons."

Hanna laughed. "Dan, I think your comment earlier that there's a remote possibility that a soaring peregrine falcon or bald eagle might spot little Maggie nursing and swoop down to pluck her from my breast for an easy meal is a bit much, don't you think?

Maggie and I feel very secure with our vigilant mountain man here to protect us."

Cresting a hill, Mirror Lake spread out like a great jewel before them. It was just as its name implied a glass-like surface, a watery canvas adorned with a reflection of the panorama that surrounded it. Dan would make camp for them, just feet from one of God's glorious masterpieces.

With the camp set, Dan hobbled the mules in the event a curious bear or cougar should happen by and spook them. Then he set out to draw a bounty of trout from the lake for his and Hanna's supper.

While Dan fished, Hanna arranged their bedding in the small tent, and then tucked Maggie, bundled in her cocoon of a down comforter, safely inside. She lit a cook fire to allow it time to burn down into coals, and then filled a canvas bag with snow from a nearby stand of pine to refrigerate the perishables.

With her chores complete, she took a seat on a weathered log and watched in silence as Dan skillfully danced a dry fly atop the crystal-clear mirror before him. Over and over, she watched his fly rod bend to the point where she thought it would break, then a Mirror Lake trout would fall for the allure of his winged offering.

"Come on, Daniel. The fire's ready. I think six of those trout is enough, don't you? Leave the rest in the lake. If you catch them all, all the bears will have left to eat will be the three of us. I'm making coffee, and I'm going to try to make you a cake in that cast-iron pot you brought if you'll get back over here and get it out of the pack for me."

As the evening faded into darkness and with the dishes from supper cleared, the two of them lay side by side on a bearskin Dan had unfurled next to the fire. Looking to the sky, they lay cuddled next to each other, gazing into the heavens as the stars one by one began to sparkle across a basalt canvas above them.

"Hanna, you know I'm going to have to take a trip when we get back, don't you? It should only be a few days, but just in case, I asked Bill Sands to check in on you while I'm gone. And by the way, I have a surprise I forgot to tell you about. Bill asked me if I would kind of be a stand-in as a reserve deputy for him from time to time if he needed help, and I said yes. You know, like I did when those boys crashed that time and I helped get them out? Well, anyway, I told him I would only do it if it was an emergency kind of thing or if he took a day off or something like that. I won't be arresting people. I'll just be kind of a backup for him if he needs help. Oh, yeah, and one other thing. I should have told you but in the rush I forgot. As a reserve deputy, he is going to have a phone guy with the county put a radio in the cabin and a radio phone so he can get in touch with me in an emergency. I told him where the key was to the cabin, and he said he should have it done by the time we get back."

"You mean they are doing it right *now?*"

"No, not right now. Maybe tomorrow or the next day, but it should be done before we get home. He said he would go with the guy, so everything will be fine. Heck, Hanna, nobody is going to mess with our things with the sheriff looking on."

"Daniel Rawlins, I know you have some things you think you need to keep quiet about, but letting some stranger into our–"

"Calm down now, sweetheart, I just forgot, that's all. It was going to be a surprise. I just wanted you to have a way to get a hold of someone if something happened when I wasn't around. I was so excited about this trip with you, I just simply forgot to tell you. Did you see that? Wow, did you see those two shooting stars just now?"

"They weren't shooting stars you saw. If you have any other surprises, you better tell me now or you're going to be seeing more stars than you ever imagined, Daniel Rawlins."

"Come on Hanna. Let's go cuddle up with Maggie. I want to get up early and take you two exploring. Maybe we can climb up the mountain tomorrow with our little *papoose* and watch the eagles. Maybe we can shoot something for supper for tomorrow night, and the three of us can hold a real Indian powwow."

"Daniel, you're really scoring points tonight! You know as well as I do that *papoose* is not a nice name for an Indian baby. Now, if you want to rethink that and drop the *papoose* part, Maggie and I would love to go with you to watch the eagles fly. And as far as the powwow part goes, that sounds like fun, too. You just never know. Afterwards, I might even consider making big medicine with Chief Daniel. After all, there are still four more of those peaks left for a future Rawlins offspring to claim. Now take me to your wigwam, Great Spirit Chief of the Canyon. I'm plumb worn out. Let's go to bed."

Early the next morning, Hanna arose to a crackling fire and a steaming pot of coffee, looking up just as Dan's naked body splashed into the frigid waters of Mirror Lake. Dan returned to camp, shivering and flapping his arms to get warm.

"Wow, now that was just a bit too refreshing," he said through chattering teeth. "I think maybe we might want to warm some water over the fire for you and Maggie. I've got goose bumps on me big enough to cook for dinner tonight."

"Daniel, I swear, if I didn't know any better I'd think you lost your mind. The snow just melted, and you're swimming in that ice pool. What in the world am I going to do with you? Now go put something warm on and I'll make you some breakfast."

They spent the rest of the day together exploring the hillsides. Dan frequently took to his lectern atop a log or rock outcropping to explain how, as the spring turned to summer, the four o'clocks now in bloom would give way to the emergence of the prickly pear cactus and the reaching tentacles of poison ivy prevalent in the area.

Interesting as it may have been for Dan, Hanna found this information somewhat unsettling when he chose a narrow ravine to stop and explain how the rattlesnakes love to lie in ambush atop rocks just like the one she happened to be sitting on.

"Dan, look over there. Look how beautiful the wildflowers are. I want to show Maggie. You go ahead if you want. I'm going to let Maggie pick some flowers."

"I think I'll go to the top of the ridge," Dan said. "I need to take a few shots with this rifle and see how it shoots. Sands put a new scope on it before I got it, and I want to see if it's sighted in right. Don't worry about a thing, I'll just be on the other side of the ridge so the shots won't scare the baby."

When Dan set out, he had full intentions of trying out the rifle Goldsmith had provided in the package at the meeting. Alone in the canyon this early in the year would provide a private environment, away from unwanted observers, to test his weapon.

Dan took up a prone position on the north side of the ridge and focused the lens of his Redfield 3x9 scope on a round, pumpkin-sized boulder resting at what he estimated was approximately 1,000 yards away on an opposing hillside.

Ever so slowly, like a cobra drawing back and about to strike, he took a deep breath then slowly exhaled as his fingertip massaged the trigger. ***"BOOM."***

The concussion of the 7.62 mm round leaving the barrel of his M-40 sniper rifle echoed throughout the canyon as he watched his first shot strike just four inches high and slightly to the left of his target. After a minor adjustment to his crosshairs, he exhaled again and squeezed, sending a second round down range, this time striking this head-sized boulder dead center.

Having satisfied himself of the weapon's accuracy, Dan rose to his feet just in time to see a covey of chucker take flight, no doubt thinking they were under attack.

As the last of the four birds flared their wings for a landing half the distance to his first target, he locked and loaded, then squeezed again, promptly removing the head of the fourth bird as its feet touched the ground.

"Well, there's dinner! By God, you can sure take that shot to the bank, Mr. Goldsmith," he gloated.

Retracing his steps with his freshly killed grouse dangling from one hand and his rifle slung on his shoulder, he soon caught sight of Hanna, and she didn't look at all pleased.

"Daniel Rawlins, if you shoot that cannon one more time…here we are in a place that can only be compared to heaven, and you go and blast away, making it sound like what it's named for, Hells Canyon. Now, you put that thing away. I don't care if we get attacked by a whole pack of mountain lions, you can just throw rocks at'em. You nearly scared Maggie half to death with all those explosions."

Having been so concentrated on shooting, Dan had forgotten how the report from the rifle could resonate in the surrounding hillsides– loud enough to wake the dead.

"Sorry, honey. I'm done. Hey, look what I got us for dinner. Have you ever eaten roasted grouse?"

"No, I can't say that I have. With all that shooting you were doing, are you sure there will be any meat left on that poor bird worth cooking? You sure as heck scared away everything else. You should have seen the eagles. They were flying everywhere."

The three of them spent a wonderful day together exploring the mountainside, with Dan going on at length about his knowledge of the plant life and the creatures that called this place home. From the outcroppings of rocks where the rattlesnakes nested to the nine-foot eagles' nests perched high in the pines, life, though mostly invisible, was present everywhere.

Up on the ridgeline a herd of elk slowly made their way down a game trail toward the lake for water as Dan readied the chucker for the spit above the fire pit. The sun's ball of fire was just disappearing behind a ridgeline off to the west when Hanna froze, then gave Dan a warning.

"Dan," she said nervously. "Don't move. There's an Indian standing over there at the edge of the trees looking at us."

Dan turned to see. Silently standing there, no more than fifty yards from the camp, a man dressed from head to toe in full Indian regalia, from his eagle-feathered headdress to his moccasin-clad feet, this was no illusion.

"My God, Hanna, I think he's a chief. Look at his bonnet. Only a chief would wear something that magnificent."

"Welcome," Dan beckoned with a wave of his hand as he rose to his feet. "Please join us. You're welcome in our camp."

Hanna, still very nervous, retreated to the tent and with one hand she moved Dan's gun belt to a spot just inside the tent flap. Then she gathered up Maggie, who was now awake and beginning to make soft but very audible crying sounds, and ventured back outside to stand next to Dan.

"I'm Dan Rawlins, and this is my wife Hanna. The little one is Maggie. She's our daughter. Please, come and join us. We're just about to make supper."

The Indian's eyes fixed on them, then slowly scanned the surroundings as if looking for others, then took one step forward out of the shadows of the trees.

"My God. With the sun on him, he looks like a monument of an 1800s Indian chief, Hanna. Have you ever seen anything so--"

Abruptly, Dan stopped. Hanna drew Maggie close to her breast as the figure began to walk silently toward them. Raising his right palm high in the air, the Indian advanced until he was within only a foot of Hanna.

Again Dan began to speak, but the man quickly dropped his hand and made a flat slicing motion across his chest, clenching his fist, clearly ordering Dan to be silent.

The man turned his gaze to Hanna, reached out, and gently lifted the corner of the quilt that covered Maggie's face.

"Her name is Maggie. She is our daughter," Hanna informed him again. "My mother was Nez Perce. My name is Migisi. You may hold her if you would like. May I ask your name?"

The Indian looked at Maggie's face, and for a moment he froze.

"You may hold her if you wish," Hanna said again beginning to hand him the baby. She wanted the old man to sense her trust.

The Indian stepped forward and accepted the bundle. Drawing Maggie close, the Indian focused on Maggie's face. Tears began to stream from the old man's eyes.

Nervously, Hanna tried to reassure the man everything was fine, but then he quickly offered Hanna back her baby.

"What should I do, Dan? I think I upset him."

"You didn't do anything, sweetheart. He just wants you to take Maggie back."

"You're welcome to stay and eat with us," Dan said again but got no response.

Slowly, the old man removed two of the smaller eagle feathers from his trailing bonnet, and with a thong he pulled from his tunic, tied the feather's quills together. He placed the bound feathers on Maggie's forehead, and without saying a word, turned and walked back to where he had first emerged from the tree line and disappeared.

"Daniel? Daniel," Hanna said, her voice trembling. "Daniel, they're gone. They just vanished like he did."

"What are you talking about? He didn't vanish. He just walked into the trees."

"I'm not talking about him, Daniel. It's the feathers. They're gone. I saw them, Daniel. They were on Maggie's forehead, and then I watched them disappear."

Neither could speak for several moments as they tried to figure out what had just happened. Then Dan broke the silence.

"Come on, Hanna. We both just probably had some kind of reaction to all the hiking. Or maybe it was the heat or the sunlight or the shadows that got our imagination going or something."

"Is that an illusion?" Hanna asked, pointing to the tree line just as a huge bald eagle with its massive nine-foot wings outstretched flew directly toward them from the exact same place the Indian had just disappeared.

As the two of them ducked in fear, the eagle flexed his huge talons, and then swerved to the right just before impact. Circling above them, lifted by the thermals of warmed air from the fire, suddenly the great bird broke left directly toward He Devil Peak and vanished.

"Did you see his eyes, Daniel?" It was crying! It was crying just like–"

"Yes, I saw. Let's get something to eat, honey. It'll be getting dark soon."

Quietly, Dan and Hanna ate the grouse he had shot earlier that day. That morning the bird had just been another creature of God's wild providence, provided to nourish His hungry children. But now, after the vision of the tearful Indian and what they both felt was his transformation from a man to an eagle, the meat they now consumed seemed flat and tasteless. After supper they turned in early but spent a restless night, their fitful dreams filled with Indians and eagles.

Dan rose just as dawn broke to the forlorn cries of a pack of hungry wolves chasing an unfortunate victim somewhere off in the distance. Echoes? Oh yes, there were lots of echoes– the favorite ballads played by these Seven Devils. Each time a wandering soul, be it man or beast, dared venture without caution from the safety of their sanctuaries, the Devils of the canyon would rosin their bows and play "the symphony of the feast."

The only sounds filling the canyon that morning as the three made their way back to Windy Gap were "Yup mule! Get up, mule! Steady Molly!" Tired, they climbed into the truck and headed for home.

Hanna sat silently with Maggie cradled in her arms, her head leaning against the window as Dan drove the few miles back to the cabin. The ghostly vision of an old Indian chief, coupled with the sudden emergence of the crying eagle now struck fear deep inside her.

"Dan, why did he cry when he held Maggie? Why did he do what he did with those feathers?"

"You have to stop it, sweetheart. We just got caught up in the moment. We'd become so enamored with all the beauty and history around us– I don't know. What we *think* we saw just couldn't have really happened. I don't know what they call it, but for some reason our minds just played a trick on us."

"You know it was real, Dan. You *know* it was real."

Chapter 11

"Come on, honey. Let's go inside and see what kind of stuff the sheriff had his boys install. It'll be nice to have a way to contact the outside world without driving into town, don't you think?"

"Don't give me that, Dan. I know what it is, and it isn't for listening for weather reports. I may not know a lot about what goes on around here, but I do know that."

"Well, lookie there. They put it right over there by the desk. It's a Motorola police radio. Now we'll know what is going on in town."

Just as Hanna headed for the bedroom with Maggie, the radio came to life. "Riggins Sheriff to unit two come in Dan! Hey, Dan boy, are you there? Unit one, to Riggins unit two, come on Dan, pick up."

Nervously, Dan keyed the mike button. "This is Dan. I mean, Unit Two, is that you, Sands?"

"Sure is, Dan. I see they got everything working out there for you. By the way, did you see the jeep yet?"

"What jeep?"

"The one parked out behind the shed. I got a hold of a surplus army jeep up in Lewiston for you to use if I need to call you out on something. I'll have Dave Pettigrew contact you in the next few days. He'll add on a garage for you to store it in. The county will pick up the bill for the material if you can help Dave put it up."

"I don't know what to say," Dan told him.

Sands laughed. "Now don't go driving it around everywhere. Have fun with it but remember it's sheriff's property. Just use it if you're doing police business. I got to go, Dan. I'll talk at you later. Riggins Unit One, over and out!"

By the time the conversation ended, Hanna had already undressed and was lying in bed next to a sleeping baby.

"Hanna, sweetheart, I'm going outside for just a bit if you don't need anything. Sands said he got me a jeep to use when I do my reserve work for him. I'll be out by the shed if you need me."

While Dan stood admiring his new toy, a 1967 converted military jeep equipped with all the bells and whistles of a police vehicle, Hanna drifted off into a restless slumber.

Tossing and turning, the visions of the old Indian's face haunted her. They had both seen this man. He had to have been there. They *both* couldn't have imagined him.

Why had he appeared? What was he trying to tell them? He had focused his attention on Maggie. Why was he crying? Why had he done that with those feathers, and then put them on her forehead? Why?

Two days later, Deputy Sands drove up behind Pettigrew, who was hauling a trailer stacked with lumber.

"Hey, Daniel, old boy, how do you like her? Pretty sweet job they did on her, don't you think? You got your own red spotlight and siren." Sands said laughing. "Even has a radio in it if you get into a big old police chase. Just remember, you can use it whenever you want, but if anyone asks, you're always on official sheriff's business.

"That Sheriff Department decal on the hood kind of gives it away. We wouldn't want anyone to think we're misusing county property, now would we? Remember, you're just a reserve deputy and not a full-time cop."

Other than an occasional wave of the hand to Sands, or someone else he recognized in town, or a brief radio check from Sands to the cabin, Dan had very little contact with anyone as March 29th, the day he was to go to White Bird, approached.

He'd already packed what he needed in a duffle bag and stored it outside in the back of the jeep. He had told Hanna that Sands had arranged for him to go down to Boise for a week to attend a class he had to take as a reserve deputy, and that it would be difficult to get a hold of him while he was away.

He'd completed all the groundwork; it was time to put the operation into motion.

Having committed the details of the dossiers of the two men to memory, Dan burned all the paperwork he had been given, except their photographs. He would be leaving before daylight. He needed to go over every detail of the plan in his mind just one more time.

Looking out the rear window of the cabin, Hanna saw Dan sitting on a ledge down by the hot spring and headed out the door with Maggie to join him.

"Hey, cowboy, how would you like a couple of good lookin' girls to join you?

Seeing Hanna had completely recovered from the somewhat quiet, depressed mood she had displayed since they had been back from the canyon, Dan's thoughts of the mission instantly vanished.

"You bet I want company! Who would have guessed I would be so lucky to find you two pretty little things roaming around here in the woods all by yourselves? Name's Dan, missy, Cowboy Dan. Who would you two little Indian darlings be?"

"Well, cowboy, my name is Migisi and this is Little Maggie. Now you just move over and give us some room!"

"Yes, ma'am. How about I cook us up a couple of those Elk steaks for dinner tonight, honey? We can have ourselves a real nice dinner before I have to leave. I'm going to have to get out of here by around four or five in the morning if I'm going to make it down to Boise for that class on time. You can sleep in if you want."

Hanna just smiled. "Stop the crap, Daniel. I might not know everything you're up to– nor do I want to– but my senses tell me that you're not going to any police school in Boise. I don't want to know what this trip is about. I just want you to be careful and for you to know how much we both love you. We don't want to ever lose you, Daniel. Just come home to us safe."

At first light, Dan walked to the helipad at the rear of the Forest Service office in White Bird. The familiar sound of the idling blades and tail rotor of an OH6 Cayuse were sounds he had heard many times before while embarking on missions in combat.

He could see the pilot, his face completely hidden behind the blackened face shield of his helmet, motioning him with a wave of his hand, then giving him a thumbs-up signal to load his gear onboard.

Seldom had he seen the faces of the pilots who had transported him on previous missions. Rarely did he ever learn their names, and never were they, under any circumstances, to learn his. They were just the tools of the mission, necessary but expendable.

Should events of a mission turn disastrous, which inevitably they sometimes did, this built-in shield of plausible deniability protected both parties. The prevention of any investigative body to uncover the identities of participants or acquire documentation of the details of an event such as this one, were of the highest priority. All that ever needed to be uttered to anyone attempting to conduct any investigation of any mission outside the company was to evoke a very simple cloaking statement and phrase: "The matter is being investigated, however due to this operation being an issue of national security we cannot make any further comment."

Once strapped in, the pilot turned toward Dan and held out a radio headset, but Dan waved him off. It would be a short flight, and he was not in the mood for conversation. To Dan, the person seated beside him in the black flight suit void of all markings or insignias, was simply a lifeless, voiceless tool necessary for his transport. He would do his job because he had agreed to do so, but he wanted to keep the world of this Black Ops pilot as far away from his life as he possibly could.

Without pressing further, the pilot gave Dan two thumbs up, pointed with both index fingers toward the windshield like a cowboy holding two six guns, then grabbed the control stick between his legs. Vaulting the chopper into the air, he barely missed the tops of the pines surrounding the secluded helipad, like a bird of prey out to hunt anything or anyone who dared to cross its path.

The black unmarked OH6 gracefully danced through the dawn-lit sky, heading east over the mountains. Furrowing the forest canopy like a silent dragon blowing down on the treetops, it skipped from ridge to ridge forging ever deeper into the Bitterroot wilderness.

With the speed and nimbleness of a hummingbird, the OH6 sprang up from the depths of a canyon. Then the pilot, this anonymous master of the sky suddenly put on the brakes. Momentarily, the pilot hovered, his blackened face shield panning the mountaintop, scanning the area to make sure they had arrived undetected.

Looking down from their lofty position, and finding the site completely deserted, they surveyed the sparsely treed ridgeline of Elks Summit directly below. Ever so gently, with the skill of a surgeon's hands, the pilot swung the helicopter 180 degrees to thread its spinning rotors within just a few feet of two massive pines, then made his descent.

After bringing the skids to rest on this makeshift mountain helipad, the pilot idled the craft just long enough for Dan to disembark with his gear.

"Good luck sir! I'll see you in five days."

Dan shouldered his duffle, ducked, scrambled to the edge of the clearing, then turned to see the pilot holding up five fingers as if he were reinforcing his deadline. With a rapid shift of the throttle, this nimble dragon sprang skyward, veered hard to the right, and vanished back into the canyon.

Silence engulfed the ridge as Dan headed out to look for a suitable location on high ground above Hoodoo Lake. If Goldsmith had been right about this location, it would take his prey some time to negotiate the winding dirt road south off of Highway 12, considerably more time than it had for the helicopter to fly in by way of the back door.

With ground moisture still high from the melting snows, Dan wouldn't have the visual advantage of being able to spot dust plumes rising off the dirt road from an approaching vehicle. But given the remoteness and silence of this location, the engine noise from any approaching vehicle would surely announce its arrival. Dan was confident he wouldn't be caught by surprise.

If the intelligence was correct, Dan figured he had plenty of time to comfortably reconnoiter the area before his target's arrival. He would hold back to a position where he could overlook the campground but maintain a sterile environment void of his tracks or anything else that may contaminate the area and give away his presence. His plan was to catch Wilburton and Crow flat-footed. He wanted them completely off guard so they would lead him directly to the stash of explosives.

Landing on the top of the ridge had given Dan the uphill advantage going in. He had little trouble packing in his gear, and a large rock outcropping at the edge of the tree line west of the lake gave him an unobstructed panoramic view of the lake's shoreline, and other possible routes his prey might take to their final destination.

Having what he felt was ample time to prepare for what lay ahead, Dan strolled down to a rocky outcropping and danced a dry fly in front of the outline of a fish taking in the sun's late morning rays. An hour later, with a small can of sterno for his smokeless fire, Dan settled back against a boulder atop a seat of pine boughs, his nimble fingers plucking the flesh from the bones of two cutthroat trout harvested from Hoodoo Lake.

Taking in the beauty of his surroundings, Dan's mind wandered time and time again back to the limited details he had been provided by Goldsmith for this mission.

True, these two men were not what anyone would define as pillars of any community. The company had gained intelligence that they were active or wannabe players in the Idaho Militia movement. And true if what the investigators had gleaned from an informant and the theft of explosives from a government facility pointed directly at Wilburton and Crow, he was dealing with some very dangerous men, but why not an arrest? Why had the company chosen to terminate this investigation by ordering a green light?"

There had to be more. They had to have had much more on these two men, or they wouldn't have chosen this resolution for what on the surface appeared to be a simple robbery by members of a radical movement.

Dan, however, was not on the "need to know" list. He was simply a tool selected to facilitate the operation, simply the knife in the drawer that would cut off the head of the snake.

As his third day dawned on the mountain, Dan became restless. Maybe the informer had been full of shit. Maybe he'd been one of the main players from the beginning, or maybe he'd just been doling out a line of crap he'd overheard from a drunken braggart.

It was late afternoon when Dan heard the sound of a laboring engine off in the distance.

From his vantage point, a mirror flash reflected from the setting sun alerted him to a vehicle as it passed through a clearing in the trees about a mile off to the north. The vehicle was moving to the east, most likely approaching the hairpin curve in the road that would head back west and dead end at the lake's campground.

It may only be an exploring fisherman heading to Hoodoo, but more likely it was his guests of honor arriving for their surprise party. Still early spring and in the middle of the week, the dirt road from Highway 12 to the lake had been snow covered until just recently. Anyone wanting to traverse this remote forest road now would certainly be coming to the campground for a very special reason, and it probably wasn't to fish.

Out from the tree line an older model Ford pickup, painted with a dull camouflage pattern, appeared. Almost at an idle, the vehicle creeped to the very end of the parking area, then slowly circled back as the driver craned his neck through his open window.

Dan's wisdom in not disturbing the virgin spring ground proved warranted, and he was now being rewarded for his effort. There was no indication that anyone had been there since before the winter snows.

The faces of Wilburton and Crow filled the lens of Dan's binoculars as he focused in on the truck's windshield. When the truck came to a halt, Crow exited the truck first, then stood by the passenger door, nervously looking to the rear, making sure they hadn't been followed.

Ever cautious of his surroundings, this man was either a highly paranoid individual or a skilled diabolical criminal. Like a rat scanning for a cat before he scurried for the cheese,

Crow slowly did a 360 degree visual scan for intruders, even making sniffing gestures, raising his nose to the air as if he could detect someone's scent.

Unfortunately for these rats, Dan was a very smart old cat who had no intention of giving away his presence, nor did he have any plans to pounce before learning where these rats had hidden their explosive cheese.

Watching the second man, Dan became convinced that Wilburton was the leader. He showed total disregard for Crow's cautious approach and exuded a posture of total arrogance as he lit a cigarette, slammed the driver's door of the truck, and walked with a belligerent gait to the pristine lake's edge.

Coughing loudly, this mucus-filled dumb ass drew back his head to spit out a wad of God only knows what atop one of the picnic tables. Then he threw what looked like an empty pint liquor bottle into the crystal clear water and began to urinate.

Wilburton was the leader, all right. He showed no respect for his partner, or for anything else. If Dan had possessed any previous reservations regarding this mission or the nefarious characters of these men, Wilburton and his partner had just erased them. Dan slowly retreated into the shadows, still keeping the two men below him in view.

He could hear the two men engage in a conversation as Wilburton unfolded a map, then pointed in the direction of the far end of the lake, an area Dan had not yet visited. Even though he had surveyed some of the vicinity, looking for the possible stash location, he had held back from the area the man was gesturing toward.

Dan had been very careful not to show any sign of his presence by restricting his movements, for the most part, to the surrounding high ground. Wherever these men had chosen to hide the explosives, they certainly weren't going to pack a hundred or more pounds of dead weight up steep slopes.

Dressed in his ghillie, Dan crept silently through the trees, taking up a position in the rocks about 200 yards from his target. After assuming a prone position on a bed of soft pine boughs, he then settled the legs of the weapon's bipod and waited for the two men to make the next move. The sun had settled off to the west, and he could hear the sounds of the trout beginning to splash in the lake in their hunt for hovering insects.

When Dan saw Crow begin to pile wood in a fire pit, he knew that the men wouldn't be going for their stash until morning. They made no attempt to set up a camp, so he felt certain that they would probably use the truck for shelter. Either they were just being overly cautious, or more likely, they may have had problems or delays on the trip in. Now it was too late to recover their booty and leave on a possibly treacherous nighttime retreat. With the back of the truck filled with C-4 explosives, the last thing these men wanted was to crash into a deer, elk, or worse in the darkness. Also, a vehicle wandering around in the woods after dark driving slow, drew not only the attention of game wardens looking for poachers, but curious cops looking for anything out of the ordinary.

All these two needed was to have a flat tire and have a cop show up to help. "Evening gentlemen, you need a hand? If you help move those explosives in the bed, I'll help you change the tire…." No, these two bastards weren't going anywhere. Not tonight anyway.

Dan was already in position when just after dawn he saw movement as Wilburton crawled out the back of the truck and ambled to the passenger door, opening then slamming it shut to wake Crow.

"Get your lazy ass up. We got work to do. I want to get the stuff and get the hell out of here. We need to get this shit to the new location and meet the others by four o'clock. I don't want to have to spend another night in the woods because of your stupidity!"

During the night while the men slept, Dan, in full camouflage, had slipped to within 100 feet of the truck so he could clearly hear everything.

Its breakfast time my little rats. It's time for you to go get your cheese, boys, Dan thought to himself.

As the two men skirted the south side of the lake in the direction Wilburton had pointed to the night before, Dan paralleled their movement, keeping hidden in the thick forest undergrowth.

"There's the place just off to the right. See that pile of rocks? The opening is back behind that brush. Help me move these logs in front. The other stuff is covered up in the back of the cave."

Dan found a raised mound of dirt directly across the lake from where the men were. He got into a prone position and watched through his rifle scope as the two cleared what appeared to be an opening to a small cave. The two men crouched down, and in single file followed each other, disappearing into the dark opening.

Wilburton appeared first, pulling on a rope handle attached to a wooden military-type ammunition box. Then Crow shoved out a second matching one.

"Get the caps and the fuse. I buried that stuff next to the back wall," Wilburton hollered toward Crow. I'll check this stuff just to make sure it's...."

Those were the last words to ever come out of Wilburton's mouth. As the man's fingers turned the thumb latch on the box, Dan slowly exhaled and squeezed the trigger. Through the eyepiece, Dan saw a red fog burst from the opposite side of Wilburton's head as the 7.62 mm slug disappeared into the cave. Wilburton lurched violently forward, then snapped to the rear as his upper torso disappeared behind a bush.

"What in the hell was that? Who the hell is...."

Crow never got his answer. Dan's second shot caught Crow squarely between the eyes, just as the man silhouetted himself against the darkened background. The shot slightly lifted him off of his feet before he fell backwards into the darkness. Dan never moved; he never made a sound for the next twenty minutes. The silence was almost deafening as he waited for his prey to bleed out from their fatal wounds.

Since last fall when the hunters and fishermen had made their final departure for the season, the only noise that had disturbed these mountaintops had been a passing thunder cloud spitting a fanged dagger-like lightning bolt into a peak or tree.

Then quietly, seemingly out of nowhere, Dan saw a young spotted fawn, then a second, followed by a doting mother doe making their way down to the lake from the ridge. Not twenty feet away, a grouse with her six hatchlings eased their way out of the brush, and headed for the shoreline in search for mountain grubs, giving little notice to the camouflaged figure they had earlier passed.

Confident that the threat had been neutralized, Dan slung his M-40 over his shoulder and made his way to the cave. Just as expected, there lay the corpse of Garvin Wilburton, face down in the mud.

How poignant, Dan thought. Even an evil man like this gives back to nature. Although it might not have been a voluntary donation, the spray of gray and red protein from Wilburton's exploding forehead now would give fertilization to the new generations of lichen and moss grasping the moist boulders surrounding the cave.

"You won't need this anymore," Dan murmured as he plucked a typographical map of Hoodoo Lake from the dead man's breast pocket. "Yep, there it is. I was right. You were the boss. You even circled the cave in red for them, Garvin old boy. The cleanup team shouldn't have any trouble finding you and Crow at all.

"Crow. Poor, stupid Crow. Dan knelt down beside Crow's body and felt for the pulse he doubted he would find, then dragged the man's corpse back to the rear of the cave. Sweeping the rock slab at the back of the cave with his palm, he found the resting place of the two mushroomed slugs. Not that he didn't trust Goldsmith or the rest of the members of the company, it was just that Dan thought it best to gather any evidence that could later tie him or his weapon to the incident.

All right. It was time to exit. He had only one thing left to do: gather his gear and make it out of the area to the pick-up point by morning for the extraction. Using the same logs the men had removed, he quickly concealed the cave's opening and headed out. After a cursory inspection of their vehicle, he used his knife to puncture a tire. Should anyone happen by, he wanted to make it appear that the vehicle was disabled and left abandoned. Then he headed for the ridge.

Cleansing his campsite and the surrounding area, he felt satisfied that even an experienced tracker would have found it very difficult, if not impossible, to find any signs that a man had ever been there.

Not long after sunup, his transportation arrived. Dan could hear what sounded like a faint, whirling buzz saw, then rising up out of the canyon he saw the image of what appeared to be a large, angry black bumblebee. He waved as it approached, then covered his face with his hat to defend himself against the rising cloud of debris as the pilot lowered the copter's tail and flared to make ready for his landing on the ridge. As he had when he'd delivered him, the OH6 pilot masked his flight by hugging the curves of the deep, surrounding canyons until the very last minute, then landed.

As the rotors slowed, the pilot cloaked in black as before, waved for him to approach.

"Beautiful morning, isn't it sir? I think you're supposed to have something for me," the pilot said, reaching his hand out as Dan hoisted his duffle bag onboard.

From inside his shirt, Dan retrieved the folded map he had taken off Wilburton and handed it to the pilot, who tucked it inside a small metal cylinder.

"Buckle yourself in, sir, I'll be right back."

As Dan prepared for takeoff, the pilot exited and walked to the edge of the clearing, pushed a button to activate the transponder device that held the map, and stashed it in a small clump of thistle.

With no further ado, the helicopter banked right, disappearing into the depths of the canyon.

"White Bird. White Bird come in. This is Black Bird. I have the messenger onboard and the package is ready for pick up."

"Black Bird, this is White Bird. Roger. Have a safe flight home. White Bird Out!"

At the same time Dan's chopper was heading west for White Bird, an Army National Guard UH-1 (Huey), commonly seen flying in the mountains, headed toward Elk Ridge.

Stopping briefly at the ridge to retrieve the transponder, the Huey continued on, landing at the campground at Hoodoo Lake to recover two very cooperative passengers and their baggage.

While Goldsmith's cleanup crew were sanitizing things at Hoodoo, in White Bird, Dan turned one last time to acknowledge the wave of his pilot, then headed to his truck. His job was over. All he had left to do was to drive the thirty miles back home to Hanna and Maggie.

Dan made a quick stop at the Sheriff's Office in Riggins as a gesture of respect for Bill Sands and to thank him for watching over his family, then headed for the cabin.

Hanna leaped out of bed when she heard the truck pull up. Cautiously, she slipped a two-inch .38 caliber revolver in the pocket of her robe. It wouldn't be like Dan to arrive that early in the morning if he had driven from Boise. That would be more than a three-hour trip just to Riggins.

Peeking through the curtain she saw Dan's truck and flung the door of the cabin open, almost knocking him off his feet as he bent to remove his boots on the porch.

"Daniel Rawlins, I could just...."

Stopping her mid-sentence, Dan planted a lingering, passionate kiss on his precious Hanna's lips.

"God, I missed you and Maggie so much! Was everything okay while I was gone?"

As he hugged her to his chest he felt a hard lump at her waist. Smiling, he reached his hand inside her robe and withdrew the weapon.

"Why, ma'am, what in the world have you and Maggie been up to while I've been gone? Here I haven't seen you for five days and you greet me at the door packing heat?"

Hanna giggled. "Just had that tucked away in case I smelled perfume on you when you walked in, Mr. Rawlins. How was school if it's okay to ask? When did you leave Boise? You must have gotten up really early."

"Oh, it was fine, boring mostly, just basic police stuff. Nothing you would be interested in. Hey, Sweetie, I have an idea. Let me get my stuff put away and I'll clean up and make you some breakfast. You can tell me all about what's been going on around here while I was gone."

The two of them spent the next couple of hours exchanging pleasantries, as Hanna told Dan what she and Maggie had been up to while they tried to pass the time in his absence. Dan suggested that since she had been cooped up in the cabin and it was going to be such a beautiful day, that the three of them drive up to Lewiston, do some shopping for supplies and maybe take in a show.

Just after eleven o'clock, as they drove through the town of Moscow, the music on the radio was suddenly interrupted.

"We are interrupting this program to bring you an important news flash from the sheriff's office in Grangeville. ABC News reports that early this morning, U.S. Marshals accompanied by an FBI special operation's team were engaged in a gun battle with two heavily armed federal fugitives in a remote area in Idaho County. The Boise County Sheriff's Office has scheduled a news conference at the Idaho County Courthouse in Grangeville at noon today.

"My God, Daniel, did you hear that? I wonder if Rick Mears was involved. God,

I hope nobody was hurt."

"I'm sure everyone's fine. They said it was federal agents, Hanna. Mears probably wasn't even involved. Anyway, if anyone from the sheriff's office had gotten hurt, I'm sure they would have said something. Now let's not let something that doesn't concern us spoil our fun. They'll tell us what happened soon enough, I'm sure."

At noon they stopped at a diner in Lewiston for lunch. A crowd had already formed in front of the television above the counter, tuned to the local news. "Look, Hanna, it's Rick Mears. Damn, look at all the cameras. I think he's going to say something. Listen."

"My name is Richard Mears. I am currently the sheriff of Idaho County, Idaho. This is all the information I have at this time.

At approximately 5:00 a.m. this morning, federal agents assigned to the FBI's Tactical Fugitive Response Team, along with officers with the U.S. Marshals Office, made an assault on an abandoned cabin in a remote canyon in the Clearwater National Forest, approximately fourteen miles west of Moose City.

"After surrounding the cabin and identifying themselves as federal officers, two suspects inside the cabin opened fire on the officers with automatic weapons. Agents returned fire, and upon entering the cabin, agents found two men mortally wounded along with a large cache of additional ammunition and explosives.

"Federal officials have told me that the two men were identified as Garvin Wayne Wilburton from Orofino and Samuel Little

Feather Crow who is reported to have been living in the town of Lowell. Both were residents of Idaho County. Agents further reported that both men were members of a newly formed militia group calling themselves The Scott Peak Watchmen.

"The United States Secret Service would not confirm or deny that this investigation had in any way anything to do with the President's scheduled upcoming fishing trip to the area next month. They would also not comment as to whether or not the President's visit would be cancelled as a result of this incident. Due to the ongoing investigation into this matter, neither the FBI, U.S. Marshal's Office, nor the Idaho County Sheriff's Office will be making any further comments at this time, except that the investigation is ongoing and that we will assist in any way possible if requested to do so.

"Since the incident took place on federal lands, the jurisdiction of the investigation will be conducted by federal investigators. I have nothing further at this time."

"Wow. Dan, do you think that had anything to do with–"

"Right now, sweetie, I think we'd better order some lunch or we're going to miss the movie. I sure am glad those government boys are doing their job, though. I sure wouldn't have wanted to run into those two nuts out in the middle of nowhere. Hey, look here in the paper. What movie do you want to go see?"

That was the last time the subject of Wilburton and Crow ever came up in a conversation between Dan Rawlins and anyone else, including Hanna.

Chapter 12

For Dan, life went on as if the incident at Hoodoo Lake had never occurred. Bill Sands had changed dramatically. The aloof, standoff behavior Dan had witnessed when Sands had first taken over for Mears had vanished, and a bond between the two men began to grow.

Summer arrived in Riggins, the snow in the mountains was all but history. Only on the highest peaks did the glacial remnants and snow remain, discolored to a brownish glaze and struggling to survive the summer heat in the shadowed crevices.

While Dan spent most of his time either scouting for game or educating himself on the currents of the surrounding rivers, Hanna found her enjoyment in spending her time totally engrossed with Maggie.

At almost nine months after Maggie's birth, Doctor Morgan made an unannounced visit to the cabin. Greeting him at the door, Hanna held out Maggie to Morgan and flashed him a smile that stopped him in his tracks.

"She said Mama! Doctor Morgan, she just looked up at me and said Mama!"

"She's a smart one, Hanna, dear. Hand me that little princess so I can give her a quick look see, and you go see if you can find that husband of yours."

"I saw him going down to the creek a little bit ago. I'll go get him."

"Don't bother going all that way. Just let me do a quick check on Maggie and I'll walk down there and find him myself."

Fifteen minutes later, Doc arrived at the creek.

"Dan? Where you at, boy?"

"Down here, Doc. I got some rocks coming loose from that last downpour of rain we had the other day. Old Mother Nature tried to give birth during the storm and turn our little hot tub into another new river. The water came down through here with a vengeance. I think there may have been a slide or, maybe one of those big pines gave way and changed the flow up the canyon."

"Dan, I need to talk to you for a minute," Doc said, turning serious.

"Sure, Doc. Just let me finish up and we can go up to the cabin."

"I think it would be better if we talk down here. You may want to keep this just between me and you." Doc took a seat on a boulder and Dan followed suit.

"A few days ago there were two men in town and they got really drunk," Doc began. "The highway patrol ended up arresting them for drunk driving as they headed out of town but one of them put up a pretty good tussle with Trooper Aubrey. Anyway, when it was over, this guy named Davis ended up with a dislocated shoulder and a broken nose.

"While I was patching him up at the jail, this guy still couldn't keep his big mouth shut. He kept going on and on about how the lying government sons of bitches had killed two of his buddies.

How they had gone to Hoodoo Lake a few weeks back and that the liars on the news said that they had a shootout with the FBI. This guy had a lot of tattoos'–, you know, that Nazi crap we see on some of these nut cases around here sometimes."

"What does that have to do with me, Doc? Why are you telling me about it?"

"Dan, you know I have never pried into your personal life. My job is just to take care of you and your family's health issues. But I still consider you a close friend. Being a doctor, sometimes I hear more than I should about things that go on around these mountains. Sometimes, way more than I need to. You know I play poker from time to time, and sometimes after a few beers the guys start flapping their lips about things that maybe they shouldn't be talking about."

Dan's blood slowly began to boil, but his former training kicked in. Having acquired the skill of maintaining his composure when confronted with difficult situations, he simply smiled. "Well, Doc, you know how some people just like to run their mouths when they've been drinking'. I wouldn't put much stock in anything you might have heard. Hell, everybody likes to tell a good story once in a while. It sounds more to me like somebody was just trying to take your mind off your cards by giving you a line of bullshit.

"I wouldn't believe everything you hear from most of those old boys, especially when they tell you they've got a shitty hand and then go ahead and raise you. You know how people lie when they're playing poker."

"You're probably right," Doc said. "I just thought I would mention it. I don't want to get a call someday that somebody you and I know real well got bushwhacked, and I sure as hell don't think that Hanna wants to end up a widow. I just want you to be careful.

You remind your friends of the old saying, 'Loose lips sink ships'. It would be a damn shame if somebody's boat sank because somebody couldn't keep their mouth shut."

Dan nodded. "I understand," he said. "But you don't–"

"Anyway, this Davis guy isn't from around here," Doc interrupted. "He and his buddy live up the mountain near Orofino. I guess they were just over in Hells Canyon fishing and getting drunk and happened to end up in our jail."

"Well, Doc, I appreciate your concern, but don't give it another thought. Come on up to the cabin and let's have a beer. Maybe I can get you drunk and you'll loosen up about some of your other patients I've been wondering about. Hell, maybe you can stick around and Hanna and I can take some of your money in a game of Hold 'em!"

Doc laughed. "I'll have that beer, but I can't stay long. I was out this way and wanted to stop by and see the three of you is all. Maybe it was just a good old boy story, and we'll leave it at that."

That afternoon Dan made an unscheduled trip into Grangeville to see his old friend Sheriff Mears. After discussing what Doc had told him, Dan returned from Grangeville driving through a torrential downpour. Looking toward the rear of the cabin, he could see that once again the waters flowing into the hot spring had breached their banks. What had always been a spring-fed creek had now turned into an angry, turbulent stream of muddy, swirling water.

Hanna laid out some dry clothing for him as he sat drinking a hot cup of coffee next to the warmth of the fire she had built in the potbellied stove.

"Daniel, when we were in town the other day, Jim Walker at the feed store said if I was interested in planting a garden, they were getting in a new line of vegetable seeds and bulbs next week. What do you think? Wouldn't it be fun to plant a garden down by the creek? Maggie and I can have our very own garden, and I can mush up the veggies for Maggie instead of buying the store-bought stuff in the jars for her. It's supposed to start getting warm next week, and if you could buy me some I would really appreciate it."

"Okay, sweetie, you sold me. Burt Summers has a rototiller I can borrow. As soon as this weather breaks, I'll till you up an area in that flat space between the shed and the creek. Just stay away from that creek until I can ride up the canyon and see what I can do to divert the water back to where it used to flow. Mother Nature might think she's the boss around here, but I'll be damned if I'm going to let her take away our hot tub. Just give me a few days and then you can plant your garden."

Dan had done as he had promised, tilling a sunlit area in a clearing among the trees.

Though the weather had improved at the cabin, rain squalls still battered the mountains off to the east, keeping him from making any attempts to ebb the flow of water that had continued to invade the boundaries of their once peaceful creek.

A few days later, the three of them went into Riggins and bought everything Hanna needed for the garden. While Hanna did her shopping, Dan stopped by the sheriff's office to visit with Dennis, who asked him to drive up the Salmon River road and check on an area far up into the canyon where a rock outcropping might have been destabilized by the heavy rains.

It was on the 4th of June, a day Dan would remember for the rest of his life. He had kissed Hanna and Maggie goodbye, and then left that morning in the jeep to do what Dennis had asked. Armed with a box of a few sticks of dynamite, he was certain that it would be a simple task to dislodge any rock hazards that existed.

Although very few people ever used the road where the outcropping was, it would be safer if the slab of rock rested on the dirt road, rather than atop some lost flatlander's vehicle.

Arriving home, Dan drove up the lane to the cabin and saw the front door standing wide open. Hanna never left it open like that. An open front door was her one pet peeve. If she'd said it once, she said it a thousand times, "Dan, close that door. You'll let in the flies and the bees."

"Hanna? Hanna, sweetheart, where are you?" he called from the stoop.

Getting no response, he yelled again, "Hanna, if you're playing games it's not funny!"

Nothing....

Remembering what Doc had told him a few days before, Dan secured his pistol from a hidden compartment under the seat of his jeep, then slowly approached the open door. Peering inside, he saw that the rear door of the cabin was also wide open and there was no one inside.

Making his way onto the back porch, he again called out for Hanna, but she didn't respond. Then, through the trees, he saw her, standing with her back to him above the creek.

"Hanna, Hanna sweetheart, it's me, honey. Are you okay?" Where's Maggie, sweetheart?"

Fear suddenly swept over him as he rushed forward to where she was standing silently, oblivious to his presence. He stopped abruptly a few feet from her. Hanna stood there in what little remained of her tattered water-soaked sundress. Her mud-covered bare feet and legs were streaked from the blood slowly oozing from multiple lacerations.

"Hanna, where is Maggie? Where is the baby, Hanna?"

Without saying a word, Hanna slowly turned and faced him. Her lower lip quivering and with tears streaming down her face, she slowly raised her hand and pointed toward the stream.

"She's gone Daniel. He took our Maggie, Daniel. God has taken away my baby." her voice was barely audible.

"How long since you saw her, Hanna?" Dan's knees began to buckle. He knew full well that her search had caused her injuries.

This man, a pillar of strength that had vowed to protect his family, a man who had learned to adapt and overcome all of life's adversities, stood totally helpless. He knew in that instant that he was no match for the cruelty of Mother Nature's diabolical fury.

With all of his inner strength, he fought desperately to maintain his composure in order to muster the courage to try to give Hanna what little hope he could. He knew full well that the speed of the flow of the swirling water gushing past them, coupled with the debris that filled the current, it was virtually hopeless that their precious little girl could have survived. But against all odds, he had to try.

"It's been a long time, Daniel. I looked all the way down the creek to where it goes into the river. She's gone. I didn't watch her closely enough, and now God has taken her from us because of my failure to protect her."

Dan stepped forward, straining to hold back his own tears as he wiped the tears from his precious Hanna's eyes. "I'm sure you did everything you could. It was as much my fault as it was yours, I should never have let either of you go down by this damn creek. I should have known what could happen. I should have bulldozed it in. If I had, this never would have happened."

Exhausted, Hanna crumpled like a rag doll into his arms. Cradling her as if she were a helpless child, Dan slowly walked up the slope to the cabin. He had little hope of finding their baby, let alone finding her alive, but he would still make a second search for Maggie.

But Hanna's physical as well as mental stability had to take precedence over a search that he knew from past experience would most likely prove futile. They had most certainly lost the baby, and he was determined to be resolute. He was going to care for what he had left. He would first take care of Hanna.

All of the creeks in the canyon, including his, eventually dumped into the swift water of the Salmon River canyon. By now Maggie's tiny body had undoubtedly reached the river and had been swept away.

Not wanting to leave Hanna alone, he did what he could to tend her wounds, then rushed her to see Doc Morgan. Two hours had passed when Doc finished the last suture on Hanna's lower thigh.

"Dan, I've done all I can for her surface wounds, but there is not much I can do for the pain she has in her heart. For the next several weeks you're going to have to put aside everything else.

"A person's mind can think horrible thoughts. For a young mother to lose a child, let alone blame herself for it, the end result of those thoughts can prove to be catastrophic. You have lost your child; you don't need to lose Hanna too."

Returning Hanna to the cabin, Dan laid his sedated wife in bed and headed for the door for one last search. Just as he was about to leave, his common sense prevailed. His duty now was not to be slogging through a raging creek bed, but to do what he could for his devastated wife.

In the event they might possibly recover Maggie's remains, the Sheriff's Office notified the Forest Service, the engineers operating the dam on the Snake River, as well as the river rafting guide services in the area about the incident. Although countless volunteers searched along the riverbanks of both the Salmon and Snake Rivers over the next few weeks, Maggie was never found.

Over the next four months, Hanna grieved, holding up for the most part. Doc had kept her heavily sedated for the first week, then slowly weaned her to light doses of Valium, and finally just placebos when she needed an emotional crutch.

Fall was in the air, and even though Dan had canceled or referred a few elk hunting clients to other guides, he still had obligations with the Sheriff's Office and agreements with the Forest Service to assist in making sure that the visiting tourists and hunters made it out of the area safely.

September had arrived, and though the rest of the country was still enjoying the beginning of fall, the mountains of the Hells Canyon area had already begun to experience their first winter snowfall.

Soon the Artic winds would head south from the Canadian border. Preparations for winter's heavy snows had to be made, and Dan had agreed to help the surrounding government agencies make them. It had been decided that because of Dan's proximity to Riggins, he would take on the responsibility for monitoring any possible highway closures to the south.

Fish and Game, along with the Forestry Service personnel were making sweeps into the high country, which included the hiking trails. The remainder of the area would be covered by a few light aircraft and two National Guard helicopters that would warn anyone on the ground who were either ignoring or were unaware of the possible danger of an impending storm. Highway Patrol, as well as the resident sheriffs and their deputized volunteer personnel to the north and east would complete the perimeter of available emergency responders.

For the last few days, the weather service had been reporting that an extreme weather front had formed along the Alaskan Aleutian Islands and had since shifted directions.

Seattle news stations reported that the center of the storm was heading southeast, and extreme weather warnings had been issued to anyone living in the upper elevations of eastern Washington State. On its current track and speed, the northern half of Idaho would be next, and Riggins sat right in the bull's-eye.

As Idahoans made their preparations, Bill Nelson was stocking up on winter supplies in his general store in Payette, Idaho, just to the south of Riggins. If the news reports were correct, this storm could provide a huge profit for him. Bill, a widower and retired police officer from Los Angeles, had owned the store for about six months, but with the culture of the locals being as such that they didn't easily accept outsiders, his business had struggled.

If the storm proved to be as severe as the reports indicated, his little store could turn from being just another small-town roadside business into a beacon of salvation, not only for travelers but for any locals who had either ignored the dire warnings or simply had not prepared.

Bill had moved to Idaho after having explored the area on previous hunting trips. Dan Rawlins, as it turned out, had guided Bill on an elk hunt, just before Bill retired, and they had become good friends. After many hours of conversations with Dan regarding the area, Bill had decided to retire in an area just north of Boise.

Had he been the young, adventurous man he'd once been when he joined the LAPD, he might have landed himself in a cabin like Dan owned in Riggins. But now, at age 62, Bill decided that it was more prudent to settle where the weather conditions proved a little less harsh. The town of Payette was a perfect fit for his needs.

Two days later, the storm struck. Massive storm clouds turned the day into an eerie twilight as the snow began to fall along the Highway 95 corridor. The previous sporadic warnings on the local radio stations, now consumed the news broadcasts.

Towns east of Seattle were without power, and those people in the higher elevations who had decided not to evacuate, were now stranded and pleading for help. The possibility of getting six to eight inches of snow to start their winter season had been welcomed, but not this, and now a feeling of desperation settled over everyone. Those who had witnessed the record storm of January 13, 1950 suddenly panicked and were regretting their decision to not heed the warnings. The storm of 1950 lasted twenty-four days, killing at least seventeen people. This current storm was taking on a weather pattern so similar to the one in 1950, only the foolish dared to ignore this one's approach.

For the remainder of that day the blizzard continued and the winds howled throughout the canyons. Just as night began to fall, flakes about one inch in diameter had reduced the visibility in Riggins from a city block to mere feet.

Dan, who had relocated Hanna to a motel room, manned the radio at the Sheriff's Office. Bill Sands had been dispatched to assist the Highway Patrol working a serious traffic accident fifteen miles north of town, leaving Dan as the only officer to safeguard Riggins. Meanwhile, one hundred miles south, a dark-colored Ford pickup pulled off Highway 95 into a parking space at the side of Nelson's General Store in Payette.

At 9:27, a frantic man dialed the operator from the pay phone at the front of Nelson's General Store.

"We need help! There's blood everywhere. You have to hurry!" the man yelled, obviously horrified by the grisly scene he'd just witnessed.

When the young Payette police officer arrived and looked behind the counter, he froze. Bill Nelson lay face down in a spreading pool of blood.

It had been just that afternoon Bill had spoken to him about staying open late that evening so he could help others in need, and now he lay dead, obviously the victim of a vicious attack. Had it not been for the storm, Bill Nelson would still be alive. He would have closed the store at six as he normally did and would be at home sipping a beer instead of bathing in his blood. This time his compassion for others had, unfortunately, placed him in the wrong place at the wrong time.

Payette Police immediately backed off, cordoning off the area and requested assistance from the Idaho State Police. Payette PD just didn't have the experience to investigate a brutal murder, let alone the murder of a retired LAPD cop.

Chapter 13

Due to the weather situation, it took almost an hour before a homicide investigator from the state police headquarters in Boise arrived at the crime scene. The burly detective exited his car and put fire to his cigar as the young officer from the Payette PD approached him and asked, "Sir, are you with the State Police?"

Blowing a cloud of smoke into the cold night air, Detective Overman paused, then, nudging his wire-rimmed glasses forward on the bridge of his nose as if he were about to begin an interrogation, he took another puff of his cigar and answered. "Yep, sonny, that would be me. Name is Overman, and I guess you kids want me to solve a murder. Where is the body?" Walking toward the officers mingling around the front door, Overman quietly mumbled to himself, "I sure hope these guys haven't messed up my crime scene."

"The victim is a police officer, Mr. Overman. I mean, he is a retired policeman from Los Angeles."

"A *cop*? You're telling me that some asshole went and killed a *cop*?"

Turning, and without further acknowledging the presence of the other three officers on the scene, Overman slipped on a pair of rubber gloves, donned booties over his shoes, and proceeded into the store.

Kneeling over the body, Overman made a quick check for a pulse– for show more than anything else. He could already tell by the discoloration of the man's face that he had been dead for quite some time.

Turning to the other men standing in the doorway, Overman's gravelly voice growled, "Has anybody, besides that officer outside, been strolling around in this place before I got here?" Satisfied with the negative response, he proceeded with his investigation. Pleased at having learned that the majority of the scene had been properly preserved, he'd asked the question to ward off anyone wanting to trail him, out of curiosity, and to firmly establish his authority over the scene.

After being assured that the person who initially called police and a patrol officer were the only additional people other than the victim and the suspect or suspects who had been in the store prior to his arrival, Overman then ascertained that neither of them had been anywhere in the store other than behind the counter where Nelson lay dead. That told Overman that the rest of the store remained fertile ground from which he might be able to glean valuable clues left behind by his perpetrator or perpetrators.

"Okay, what's this about the victim being a cop?"

"I got this out of his pocket," a young officer responded, handing Overman a black leather wallet containing Bill Nelson's retired police ID card and badge.

"All right, you all go on outside and get a doughnut or something, and let me do my work. Let me know when the coroner gets here, but stay outside until I've had a chance to look around."

Slowly and methodically, Overman scanned each of the three aisles, mentally noting anything that looked out of place. Finding nothing obviously amiss, he entered the men's restroom and froze. Someone other than the dead man had been in there, and it hadn't been that long ago. Overman noted that someone had urinated in the toilet and hadn't flushed. He also noted what appeared to be the tracks from a wet pair of muddy shoes leading from the doorway to the stool.

"Any of you boys happen to come in here and take a piss before I got here?" he shouted loudly over his shoulder.

Receiving a negative response, he continued through the store, finding that traces of the muddy footprints led up to the counter, then turned and made a trail behind the counter. Looking up, he saw an empty space on the shelf where bottles of liquor were neatly displayed. Scanning further, he noted a partially empty box of ammunition with four loose bullets scattered on the floor. Boxes of bullets were stacked neatly in the glass case under the cash register, only one stack was shorter than the others– the stack of .38 caliber handgun bullets.

Turning toward the counter he noted that the cash drawer had been emptied, and just below the counter, slightly hidden from view, he spied a brown Hoyt holster, the brand of holster old cops commonly used for their off-duty weapons.

Confident he could accomplish little else until his crime scene team arrived to photograph the scene, he exited the store and gathered the other officers for a briefing.

"First of all, gentlemen, you all did a fine job. You didn't mess up a thing. Unless we find out differently, or unless Officer Nelson sits up to tell me I'm wrong, this is what I think happened here.

"Our perp came in the front door and moved off to his left, putting the shelves between him and Mr. Nelson. From the looks of the muddy tracks from his tennis shoes, he proceeded to the bathroom where he took time to pee. From there he made his way to several locations around the store before he ended up back at the counter in front of the cash register. Then he walked back behind the counter where it looks like he might have taken Mr. Nelson's handgun. Somewhere along the route, either before he went behind the counter or when he may have seen Nelson going for his own gun, this weasel son of a bitch put at least one or maybe two bullets square in the back of Mr. Nelson's cranium, dropping him right where he stood. Our friend then left the store and fled into the dark, snowy night.

From the looks of the footprints and water on the floor of the bathroom, our suspect did some walking in a muddy area. But the front parking lot is paved, as well as partially shoveled. Have your people take a good close look around the building for fresh tire tracks, other than your own, or any other evidence that might help us identify our perp. Other than that, there is very little else we can do here tonight.

"Once we take care of a few more details, the coroner can remove Nelson's body, and if you've finished interviewing the reporting party, that's it for this evening. I'm wet, tired, and mad as hell over what this bastard did to one of ours. I'm going home, have a few drinks, and hit this first thing in the morning when I'm fresh. Goodnight, my brothers. Now you all be safe."

After everyone filed out, Overman trudged to his vehicle and keyed the radio mike.

"Dispatch, this is unit H2. Put out a notice to all agencies that a robbery homicide took place this date in the town of Payette. The victim of this crime was identified as a retired Los Angeles police officer. The crime was committed at the Nelson General Store on Highway 95 sometime around nightfall. We have no vehicle description at this time. The suspect may be wearing tennis shoes with a horizontal squiggly line pattern on the soles, approximately size 9. Suspect or suspects are armed and dangerous with one or more handguns in their possession, one possibly a .38 caliber revolver. Suspect may also be in possession of a large amount of cash as well as one or more pint-size bottles of Ten High brand whiskey. Direct any information to our homicide office, attention Detective Overman.

"That's all, Betty. I'll be enroute home if you need me. Goodnight!

"Oh, Betty, one more thing, you might want to call a few of the departments up north as well as the Canadian Authorities and alert them just in case this guy gets the notion to head up to Canada. Unit H2 out!"

Just as Dan was about to leave the office to check on the road conditions, the telephone rang. It was the Idaho County Sheriff's dispatcher in Grangeville.

The senior dispatcher passed on the information regarding the robbery/murder that evening in Payette.

When Dan heard that a retired LAPD officer by the name of Bill Nelson had been the victim, Dan went limp, dropping back into his chair. After losing Maggie, and now to lose a good friend within months of each other, all he could think was, what in the hell could happen next? Tomorrow he would find out more about what had happened in Payette, but now he had not only the townspeople to look after but travelers in the area as well.

Dan was instructed to pass on the information to anyone of authority as well as snow removal crews, in the event they came upon any unusual or abandoned vehicles along Highway 95 during the night. State Police advised that there would be additional information to follow, however, there was still no suspect or vehicle information available.

It had been almost two hours since Randal Holmes had pulled the trigger of the gun that ended Bill Nelson's life, but only twenty minutes since the State Police put out a BOLO (Be on the lookout) message to other agencies.

Holmes had only passed a few other vehicles on his route north. Given the snow- covered roads, travel by those willing to venture out into the storm had been sporadic, but now the severity of the storm had ebbed. Running on the adrenalin rush from the murder, the killer's confidence was up and so was the weight of his foot on the accelerator.

Just after 2:00 a.m., Dan advised dispatch that he was retiring to the motel. He had only seen five or six vehicles driving around town during the last several hours, and every one of those he recognized as locals. The probability of anyone else stirring around was pretty low. If an emergency came up they could contact him there.

By dawn, the storm had moved on. It was now tracking north and east of Riggins. The residents could take a breather, at least until the next tempest.

Just before 6:00, Dan met up with Deputy Sands at the office. Sands, too, had been up most of the night assisting the Highway Patrol with accidents and stranded motorists.

As they discussed what had transpired in Payette, Sands told Dan that due to the traffic accident on North Highway 95, it was highly unlikely that the shooter had made it into their area. At the crash site, he had waved a few locals through, and the only additional traffic he'd seen were a couple of motor homes occupied by some elderly people that had either gotten themselves lost or had packed up in fear of becoming stranded.

"Riggins Sheriff's Office, do you have a copy? Riggins come in, over!"

"Riggins here, Hattie. This is Self. Go ahead."

"Bill, we just got a call from the Highway Department. Dick Stone, one of their plow drivers, is about seven miles south of the bridge at the Little Salmon. He said he just came across a wrecked pickup truck that went over the bank, and it's lying upside down on the embankment next to the river.

"The site is just a few hundred yards north of the road leading to Ben Davis's ranch. Bill, he said that it's pretty bad. The driver is dead, and he can't get to the passenger.

I've already dispatched an ambulance, and I'm getting ready to call a wrecker. Let me know if you need anything else when you arrive on the scene. The Highway Patrol has already been notified, but their closest unit is thirty miles away, so it looks like you'll probably be first on the scene. Oh, and by the way, he said there's lots of money lying all over the place, and he found a gun next to the truck."

"10-4, Hattie. Dan Rawlins is here with me. We're on our way. Riggins out."

Keeping in mind the information they had received the night before concerning the murder in Payette, Sands advised dispatch to contact the plow driver and tell him not to disturb anything at the crash site. He also told her to contact the State Police and give them a heads-up, to inform the detective who had issued the BOLO, and to ask if they had any available units.

When Dan and Sands approached the scene, the blend of the yellow flashing lights on the snowplow, combined with the red lights of the police unit, cast an eerie glow throughout the snow-covered canyon. With the snowplow parked northbound on the shoulder, they could see the driver silhouetted, waving his arms frantically in the air, obviously shaken by what he had seen.

"Mr. Stone, are you okay?"

"They are down there, Sheriff. I just happened to see the glow from the headlights shining up on the embankment and something moving on the other side of the river or I probably wouldn't have stopped. When I got to the edge of the road and looked down I saw the truck. I went down to see if I could help, but they're both dead. Jesus, Sheriff, there's money blowing around all over the place, and there's a gun on the ground about halfway down the embankment."

"Did you touch anything? The gun, or anything else?"

"No, Sheriff. I reached in the window and checked for a pulse on the driver, but Jesus, the man is almost frozen stiff. I could see the legs of a girl on the passenger side, but her body is crushed up under the dashboard. Other than that, I haven't touched a thing. Jesus, he must have rolled that thing several times before it hit that big rock. They didn't have a chance."

"Dan, go lay out some flares down the road to the curve." Sands said. "I think we might be here for a while. It looks like we might have our murder suspects. I'm going to contact the State Police and give them an update, go down and take a quick look around the vehicle, and then we'll just preserve the scene and stand by and let the State boys decide what they want us to do."

It was almost 9:00 by the time Detective Overman arrived at the scene. The Highway Patrol had taken control, and other than standing guard over the crash site, there wasn't much else Dan could do until the State said it was okay to recover the victims and the vehicle.

Having been briefed, Overman and Sands headed down the embankment to view the scene and gather evidence.

Dan, while only playing a supporting role in the investigation, began to scan the surrounding area to see if anything else had been thrown from the vehicle as it careened off the roadway.

Lying in a snowdrift approximately 100 yards from the wreck Dan found what appeared to be a baby bottle along with a few cans of baby formula and various articles of clothing.

Oh my God. What the maintenance driver had said suddenly struck him.

"If I hadn't seen some movement up on the embankment, he wouldn't have seen the wreck."

"My Dear God," he thought. Was the movement he saw some animal scavenging the wreck site early that morning? Was there a child in the vehicle, possibly ejected, that was now becoming a meal for a predator?"

Dan spotted a log pinned in the rocks that he could use as a bridge to the opposite bank. Not taking time to alert Sands or Overman who were working with the wrecker operator to gain entry to the vehicle, Dan crossed the river and headed up the other embankment toward the tree line. Slowly searching the snow covered ground for any tracks, Dan didn't see the man until he stepped from behind a large pine.

"Hold it right there. Sheriff's Department," Dan ordered, drawing his gun. "Don't you move!"

An elderly Indian dressed in native clothing stood just feet in front of him. Dan moved slowly to the rear and off to the side so he could attain a better tactical position. Without saying a word, the man extended his arms. The Indian was cradling what appeared to be something wrapped in a sleeping bag.

"Just put it on the ground and step back!" Dan ordered.

Ignoring the order, the Indian slowly stepped forward, continuing to offer what he was holding to Dan. As Dan nervously assessed his next move, he heard emanating from the bundle the faint crying sounds of a baby.

Cautiously, Dan stepped forward and gently pulled back a corner of the wrapping. To his complete amazement, his eyes fell upon the reddened face of an extremely small baby. Connecting the dots of what he had seen on the opposing side of the river, Dan snatched the baby from the Indian's arms.

"We need to get this child out of the cold. You just follow me. We are going to have to ask you some questions," Dan told the old man.

"Sands, hey Sands!" Dan yelled, hurrying down the hillside. "Sands, I found a baby. It's alive. This Indian here found a baby. I think it's from the wreck!"

Sands and Overman immediately looked in Dan's direction. "What in the hell did you just say?" Overman yelled back.

"I said this old Indian found a baby that I think may have been thrown from the wreck, and he was up there on the hillside taking care of it."

"What old Indian? What in the hell are you talking about?"

"That guy right over there!" Turning, Dan pointed to what was now just a vacant area at the tree line.

Continuing up to the highway, Dan gave custody of the baby to a State Trooper and ordered him to take the child into Riggins to Doctor Morgan's office. Then, he quickly turned and retraced his route back to where he had seen the Indian with Sands and Overman slipping and sliding in hot pursuit behind him.

"Okay, where the hell is this Indian? Why in the hell did you let him get away from you?" Overman lambasted.

Without responding, Dan began to retrace his steps to where he had last seen the Indian standing. "There's nothing here. Where in the hell did he go?" Dan said, baffled.

"Nobody could have gotten away in this snow without leaving any tracks."

The only tracks Dan could find, close to where he had seen the man, were his own and the tracks from a large bird. They were, unmistakably, the tracks of an eagle, evidenced by the deep puncture marks from its sharp talons.

"He was right there. The Indian was holding the child in his arms, Bill. I swear he was standing right there."

"Come on, Dan. Let's get back down the hill. We can look around for this Indian later. He probably just heard the noise and came down the hill and found the baby on the bank. We can go look for him after we clear up this other mess. Come on, Dan. Let's go. I need your help."

The initial investigation at the scene revealed a multitude of facts that would catapult Overman's case to a rapid resolution. Initially, without witnesses or any other suspect or vehicle information, solving Nelson's murder would have been extremely difficult at best.

If the crime lab wasn't able to identify a suspect by fingerprints possibly left at the scene, charging, let alone convicting, someone for wearing tennis shoes with a tread pattern matching those at the scene would be impossible. But because of the accident, that wasn't the case.

It was several hours later before the Idaho County Coroner removed the two victims, a man and a woman, from the truck. The male, possibly twenty to thirty years of age, had been impaled on the steering column, which had resulted in his immediate death.

The female passenger, however, looked much younger. They estimated her age to be no more than fifteen to twenty years old. The impact had thrown her forward onto the floor of the vehicle. The dashboard had collapsed, crushing her against the inside of the firewall. The temperatures of the victims, now almost frozen, left no doubt that the accident had taken place several hours before it was discovered.

Searching the vehicle as well as the surrounding area gave way to a virtual treasure trove of not only information on the victims' identities, but overwhelming evidence of their involvement in Bill Nelson's murder.

A total of six hundred and fifty-three dollars in currency was collected from the ground around the vehicle. A Colt 2" revolver with two spent casings in the cylinder was recovered from the male's waistband, and a Smith & Wesson 4" Colt Python revolver was recovered sticking out from a snow bank next to the vehicle. On the dead man's feet they found the matching tennis shoe soles that had made those muddy footprints in the store.

A records check revealed that the Smith & Wesson was registered to a Dan Nelson in Los Angeles.

The coroner at the scene recovered a wallet from the male with an Illinois driver's license in the name of Robert Cutter, age twenty-six. And in the female's purse they found a student photo ID card with the name Leandra Morton from a junior high school in Long Island, New York, along with some paperwork indicating that she had stayed at a women's shelter in Little Rock, Arkansas, eight days prior to the accident. The date of birth on the ID card indicated that she had just turned sixteen, one month earlier.

The license plate on the truck belonged to a 1963 Dodge farm truck registered in Oklahoma, but the vehicle identification number on the truck involved in the accident came back to a 1982 Ford F-150 pickup truck reported stolen from Memphis, Tennessee, ten days prior to the accident. And last but not least, lying in the snow approximately ten feet from the vehicle they'd found the crushed remains of a cardboard box with the shipping label still intact. Its destination had been Nelson's General Store, Payette, Idaho. Found inside the box were two boxes of .38 caliber ammunition with matching lot numbers to those remaining at the scene of the murder, along with three bottles of Ten High whiskey.

With the scene and evidence secured, Sands and Overman agreed that with Overman having his hands full with the murder investigation and the Highway Patrol investigating the double fatal accident, the best assistance Sands' office could give was to first make arrangements for the welfare of the surviving baby.

Sands' office would also be responsible for trying to locate and notify any relatives of the victims once their identities were confirmed. They would then need to coordinate any arrangements required to reunite the baby with its blood relatives, once proper custody could be established.

With their mission completed, Dan followed Self back to Riggins. Driving back, it hit him like a freight train. He had seen that old Indian before! His mind suddenly flashed back to the time he had been camping with Hanna and Maggie in Hells Canyon.

That same Indian had appeared out of nowhere. That same Indian had held Maggie in his arms. That same Indian with tears streaming down his face had frightened Hanna that day. Dan remembered those eyes!

Dan strained to remember every detail of his previous encounter with the old Indian so that he could accurately relay the description of the man and the circumstances to Sands when he got to the office. But as he began to tell Sands of the encounter, Sands raised his hand and stopped him.

"Dan, I saw the tracks up on the hillside just like you did. There weren't any footprints in the snow trailing back into the trees from where you found that baby. Moreover, we didn't see any footprints, except our own, leading from the crash site to the other side of the river, or down from the trees on the opposite bank to the crash when we first arrived.

"All right. You say he was there, and then he vanished. I believe what you say, but I have no plausible explanation for any of it. The important thing is the baby is alive, regardless what occurred. With all that has happened, do you really think we need to muck up the water by throwing your encounters with an old Indian we can't find into the mix? Whatever his reason for being there just doesn't matter. By his actions, we can assume his only goal was to protect that child, not to gain any notoriety by becoming a hero in a police report.

"So I think for the good of everybody concerned, when you write your supplemental report about finding the baby on the other side of the river rolled up in the sleeping bag, you just leave it at that. There is nothing to be gained by feeding the local news reporters any more information than they will already have.

"Now do me a favor, and go over to Docs, and see what information he has on the baby. I'll run the names of the victims through Illinois and New York and see if I can come up with a relative or someone who knows either one of them. Call me when you get any more information so we can wrap this thing up and get that baby to where it belongs. I want to go home and so do you. It's been a long forty-eight hours for both of us."

Chapter 14

"How's the baby, Doc? Are there any injuries?" Dan asked as he took a seat in Doc Morgan's office.

"She's just fine, Dan, though I don't know how," Doc admitted. "The trooper said you found her on the other side of the river from the crash? She sure is one lucky little girl. Because someone wrapped her up in that sleeping bag, the thick insulation cushioned her. My God, Dan, thrown that far from a vehicle, landing on those rock outcroppings, spending, who knows how long in that freezing temperature, and she looks like she just woke up from taking a nap in a warm bassinet."

"How old do you think she is, Doc?"

"It's hard to say, but she can't be more than a few weeks, maybe a month, tops. Other than some reddening around her face and a tad bit of frostbite on her left hand, there isn't a mark on her. It's simply amazing. Did Sands tell you what he wants me to do with her?" Doc asked, his expression serious. "Were those poor people in the wreck from around here? We really should get a hold of the family, not only for the obvious reasons, but just in case she has any medical history. She looks like she's in good health, but sometimes you never know without any history on the parents."

"Right now, Doc, the only information we have is that the girl who was killed in the crash might be from New York and the young man from Illinois. Bill is running down what few leads we have, but with something like this it could take hours, if not days, before we can confirm or even contact next of kin.

"Can you take care of her, Doc or do you know anyone who can for the time being? I sure don't want to turn such a little one like this over to the state child protective services right off the bat if we don't have to. From the experience I had with them when I was a kid, it would be like sending a puppy to the dog pound. It would probably only be for a short time, Doc, if you can think of anyone who might be able to care for her in the meantime."

"Well, now that you mention it, Dan, I think I know just the perfect person for the job. She's a perfect mother and loves children. I bet if you explain our situation to her she would be overjoyed to help this precious little girl until we can find her loved ones. As a matter of fact, I think you already know her. Her name is Hanna Rawlins."

"Oh my God, Doc. I couldn't. Hanna is barely getting over our losing Maggie. Jesus Doc, who knows how she would react?"

"Daniel, I know the both of you, and I especially know the emptiness Hanna feels in her heart from losing Maggie, but she still has those motherly instincts. Go and talk to her. Let Hanna make this decision. I know you want to protect her, but keeping her from moving on with her life is not protecting her. Someday she will have to bury the tragedy with Maggie and begin living again. Taking care of this little girl, if only for a few days, may be just the medicine she needs to begin healing. The mind and the heart are truly magical things, Dan. This might be the very thing you both need. Just have a little faith."

An hour later, Hanna led Dan into the rear of Doc's office. "Where is that precious little girl, Doctor Morgan? You better not have asked anyone else, to take care of this poor little thing!"

"No sirree, Hanna," Doc retorted. I wanted just the right lady to take care of her until they find out what's going to happen to her."

Gently unwrapping the comforter Doc had used to replace the sleeping bag, Hanna got her first glimpse of the little baby girl. Weighing in at just over eight pounds, she appeared irritated by the bright lights, illuminating her strange new world.

"Oh, my. Don't be scared, little one. My name is Hanna. I'm going to take care of you just like your mommy. Everything is going to be okay. I'm going to take care of you, my little angel." Hanna leaned forward and placed her warm lips gently on the baby's forehead. At the same time, the child, attempting to focus on the face above her, raised her tiny bandaged hand and touched Hanna's cheek, acknowledging her presence.

"Well, nothing's ever going to happen to her as long as she's with me, Doc. I'll take care of her just like she was my little Maggie. Now as for you, Mr. Rawlins, go warm up that jeep. This baby needs a warm bottle of milk and a safe place to sleep while they try to find her family. I still have some formula and all of Maggie's things that I saved at the cabin, so we can go straight home."

Hanna sounded more like a military commander ordering his troops into battle than his grieving wife. Dan shrugged his shoulders in total disbelief at the way Hanna had reacted to the situation, but immediately did as he had been told. Dan gave Doc a somewhat tentative smile, then headed toward the door. "Women," he mumbled. "Who will ever understand women?"

Hours turned into days, then days into weeks as officers with the New York State Police tried to run down leads on Leandra

Morton. The coroner's office autopsy report stated that the dead girl had recently given birth.

A comparison of Leandra Morton's blood and that of the baby confirmed that she was in fact the mother. However, the blood examination also confirmed that Robert Cutter was not the baby's father. The baby's blood type and Robert Cutter's blood type ruled him out as the father.

The follow-up with New York authorities revealed from school records that a single woman by the name of Naomi Morton was listed as the mother of Leandra. Also found was a coroner's case file for the "deceased" Naomi Morton. The cause of death was listed as an acute heroin overdose.

The report named Leandra Morton, age 14, as Naomi's daughter and *only* next of kin. Another record stated that Naomi Morton had been discharged at the age of eighteen from an orphanage in New York State, but the file had been sealed by the court so they could provide no additional details.

School records from where Leandra's ID card had been issued revealed that it had been over a year since she had attended class there. The school had no record of her mother's death, and when Leandra stopped attending school they had just assumed that she and her mother had moved without giving a forwarding address.

In short, police officials in New York stated that they had run into a dead end as far as locating any living relatives was concerned. They advised that they would keep the matter open just in case someone came forward inquiring about Leandra or her baby, but otherwise there was nothing more they could do.

Robert Cutter, however, proved to be a different story all together. The Illinois Department of Corrections knew both

Robert Cutter as well as his father. Robert's father, Dwayne Cutter, was currently on Death Row, and had been for almost four years.

The report stated that Dwayne Cutter had been convicted and sentenced to death for the brutal murder and dismemberment of Robert's mother Susan, as well as another man.

According to that report, he was currently waiting to be executed at the Menard State Prison in Chester, Illinois.

Robert Cutter, on the other hand, had been in a juvenile corrections facility at the time, serving one of his many sentences for burglary, car theft, and selling drugs. Records indicated that he was currently wanted for escaping from a minimum security facility in southern Illinois three weeks prior to the wreck in Riggins.

When Sands called the Illinois State Prison to have them notify Robert's father of his death and inquire as to what they wanted the state of Idaho to do with Robert Cutter's remains, the voice on the other end of the phone broke out in laughter.

"Sheriff Sands, sir, I believe I can speak for the warden regarding your situation. The State of Illinois Department of Corrections, with all due respect for his passing, couldn't give a shit what you do with that little asshole's remains. Maybe you could stuff him and hang him on the wall, for all we care you could stick him up over one of your jail cells like one of them elk or deer heads you guys collect. At least there is one thing for sure, he isn't going to be wasting any more taxpayers' money by sitting in jail, is he?"

That was the last time the Idaho County Sheriff's Office had any further contact with either the State of Illinois or the State of New York regarding the matter. The issue of the surviving infant's future was now the problem for the State of Idaho to handle.

Having nothing further to go on, Overman closed the case on Bill Nelson's murder. Though Overman was somewhat saddened that this baby's young mother had lost her life, his sympathy for the driver, Robert Cutter, fell somewhat short.

When Sands updated Overman regarding their office's research on the backgrounds of the two victims, Overman paused for a moment, hardened by his years in Homicide he said, "It's truly a shame about the young girl, Leandra but I think that cop killing son of a bitch Robert Cutter certainly got his just due, don't you? Yep, it couldn't have been more appropriate. He got sent straight to hell, right here in our very own Hells Canyon!"

Dan, Bill Sands, and Overman, along with a representative from the Los Angeles Police Department attended Nelson's Funeral. Bill Nelson's relatives had been notified of the circumstances of his death.

Although they had expressed their sadness for his passing, finding any of his relations who wanted to step up to the plate to be responsible for the cost of his funeral was another thing completely. Nelson's remains had been kept in refrigeration for almost two weeks before the county realized that the duty to bury the man would fall on them.

Other than fielding a barrage of questions from Nelson's family regarding the distribution of the dead man's assets and the disposition of the real estate he had purchased in Payette, they had no interest at all in spending any of their newfound wealth on his funeral.

When the word got out to the surrounding police and sheriff's departments that a fellow officer now laid abandoned by his kin, his brothers in blue came through for Bill Nelson in spades. With very little persuasion, a local funeral director donated a first-rate casket, as well as all of his services, including the gravesite for Bill's going-away celebration of life. More than fifty officers attended in uniform from the various agencies. They sent Officer William Nelson off with an honor guard and a twenty-one-gun salute any police officer would have been proud of. All who attended decided that Dan, having known Bill better than anyone else in the area, should be given the American Flag that had draped his coffin, as well as his Smith & Wesson revolver recovered from the wreck.

With the knowledge that the little girl in his and Hanna's care had no surviving relatives, a decision over her fate would soon be made as well.

If the State of Idaho were given the facts of the case, baby Doe would certainly be processed as an orphan, and the mountain of red tape would begin. Considering the baby's young age, the chances of her being adopted were extremely high. The list of waiting prospective parents was lengthy, not only in Idaho but the surrounding states as well, but Dan and Hanna Rawlins's names were not on that list.

During the last few weeks, Dan had seen a sparkle return to Hanna's eyes that had been absent since the loss of their baby. Just as she had been with their precious Maggie, Hanna never strayed far from Baby Doe's side, ever present to attend to her every need.

Then it hit him. Why shouldn't they adopt the baby? It would be the answer to the prayer Hanna had so often made to God– the prayer that He might one day return her baby.

Hanna swung the front door wide open when she saw Dan's jeep barreling down the lane in a cloud of dust. Her heart suddenly sank. "Oh no, Lord, he's coming for the baby!" Turning, she quickly ran to the bedroom to gather up the little girl she had become so deeply attached to.

"Hanna? Hanna, honey, I want to ask you something very important," Dan called as he came through the front door. "Where are you, sweetheart?"

"I'm here, Dan, in the bedroom with the baby. Is something wrong?"

"Hanna, I just spoke to Bill Sands and Doctor Morgan." he said, entering the bedroom. "They can help us if you say its okay."

"If what's okay Dan?" she questioned, fearing what the answer would be.

"If it is okay with you, they think they can help us adopt the baby."

Slowly, Hanna dropped to her knees with the infant clutched closely to her breast, her heart racing, "We can adopt her, Daniel? Nobody wants her? Tell me it's true, Dan. Oh my God, Daniel tell me it's true we can keep her."

"We have to shave a few corners, Hanna, but with the people I know and the connections they have, Bill said if we want to do this they could pull a few strings. We're going to have to keep it a bit under the radar if this is what we decide to do."

"What do you mean, have to keep it under the radar? Is what we're doing going to get us into trouble?"

"Just let me explain, sweetheart. You know I can't tell you everything about my past, but what I can say is that I know people in the government that owe me some favors, and I think it's time I collect on a few. All I want to do is give you back your happiness. I want so much to help God answer your prayers."

Late into the evening, Dan and Hanna formulated a plan. Dan explained that there was a list of people waiting to adopt a baby, and some of them had been waiting for years. They would be very upset, to put it mildly, if they ever found out about any of this. The state could step in at any time if a complaint was lodged by another couple who had seniority on the list. This whole thing could come to an abrupt halt before it went anywhere.

Dan explained that records of birth and death could be amended if the right people had access. Further reports and records sometimes disappeared or could be substituted if you have loyal friends. Only one thing that might come up that could arouse suspicion. The baby needs a name as well as a birth certificate.

It was then, that Hanna realized what Dan had been trying to explain to her. "Well, why would that be a problem, Daniel? Maggie's birth certificate is right over there in the hope chest."

"Hanna, I think Maggie, would be very proud to have our new little baby Maggie named after her, don't you? Very proud indeed."

That evening, as night was about to fall, the screeching sound of a male eagle summoned Dan and Hanna to the entrance of the cabin. Standing only a few feet away, they watched as this majestic bird bowed his head, acknowledging their presence. Slowly, he lifted his head, spread his massive wings, and took flight, circling the cabin, finally coming to rest on the ridgeline of the roof. As a sentinel, his posture signaled to all that he would never again abandon his post. He would never again fail to protect Maggie, for Maggie had been reborn.

Although they had some concern that a few people close to Dan and Hanna would ask questions, he was certain most would have no problem taking an oath of silence to protect their secret. In the small town of Riggins, people were like a big family, and what went on in their family was nobody's business but their own.

From that day forward, not a soul ever again mentioned their baby disappearing. Dan and Hanna would return to a place in time where joy would flourish once again.

Chapter 15

Over the next fifteen years, Hanna became such a doting mother, it was not uncommon for the townspeople, whose children attended school with Maggie, to comment that the cocoon Hanna had surrounded Maggie in was too protective. Given Hanna's vigilance, no one imagined that the young girl would be able to flourish as much as she did. Hanna would always hover close by, always poised, ready to pounce like a mother cougar to protect her young should anyone enter their realm.

By the fifth grade, Hanna had spent so much time working with Maggie on her spelling assignments, none of the other children could come close to competing with Maggie at the yearly spelling bee at Riggins Elementary or anywhere else in Idaho County.

The girl also loved to recite poetry. On one occasion in her high school class, she asked her teacher if she could recite one of her favorite poems, Emily Dickinson's, "If I Can Stop One Heart From Breaking." Only this time she wanted to recite it in French.

Not wanting to appear ignorant of her inability to speak the language, her teacher suggested that she recite it in English so everyone would better enjoy it. Maggie, however thought not.

"The French language has such a beautiful resonance, don't you think, Mrs. Wilson?"

Mrs. Wilson wasn't about to let anyone in the room know that she had no clue, whatsoever that Maggie had flawlessly delivered the verses.

"Hell's bells," Mrs. Wilson had once commented to another faculty member, "I didn't recite that poem in *English* as well as Maggie Rawlins just did, and I was reading it from a college textbook. My God, that girl did it in French, from memory!"

As involved as Hanna had been in Maggie's education, Hanna did not act alone. Although he wasn't present at every twist and turn of Maggie's young life, Dan was still unmistakably there, behind the scenes, molding her character in other areas. He had taught her everything he knew about the ways of the forest and its countless inhabitants. Before she turned ten, Maggie could not only track a mouse from a grain sack to its nest but an elk into Canada if she had had a mind to.

But Dan and Maggie failed to have one thing in common, their personal convictions about taking or granting life to all of God's creatures.

In Dan's opinion, God had put game on this earth to nourish the hunter. Killing an animal for food was part of the circle of life. Like the eagle was given the vole for sustenance, man was given the trout and the elk. Maggie, on the other hand, felt that even a cockroach scurrying from the light had its place, and if possible should be allowed to live its life unmolested.

Although their two philosophies did not run parallel, their love for one another created a mutual understanding for both of their viewpoints, so the subject was seldom discussed. With their compromise clearly established, Dan would hunt the wild animal while Maggie would hunt the wild rivers. Maggie loved the wild creatures, and they loved her back. Dan, in that regard, was on his own.

By the time she was twelve, Maggie Rawlins could run the white water of the Salmon River with the best of them. Dan had taught Maggie the location of every submerged boulder ten miles east of their cabin to the point of the confluence where the Salmon met the Snake in Hells Canyon and beyond.

At age fifteen, with her knowledge and technical expertise, she had developed such a reputation on the river, she had become the go-to-guide for advice.

By the age of seventeen, her knowledge and skills had been refined to the point where it was considered foolish, for anyone to attack these rivers before asking Maggie about current river conditions. For many who thought they knew better and chose to ignore this advice, it proved to be a recipe for disaster.

More than one adventurer, who had dared to launch their crafts into the turbulent whitewater of either the Salmon or the Snake without first gleaning what they could from Maggie, ended up leaving town with little more than their lives. And those were the lucky ones. Many a shattered kayak, once filled with gear, had been found scattered along the banks of the rivers, their ghostly remains screaming out to others who dared, "Next time, you'd better ask Maggie Rawlins!"

No matter where the purists who wanted to challenge the "real white water" gathered, you would hear "Maggie Rawlins's" name mentioned. Like her father, she had become the very best at almost everything she tried.

Maggie graduated from high school with a 4.0 grade average at the age of seventeen, a year ahead of her peers. Only one thing had always saddened Maggie. She lacked friends her own age. Maggie wanted to make friends, but others were jealous of her accomplishments and kept her at bay.

Jealousy was not a part of Maggie's makeup, nor did she ever come to understand it. She just loved life and did everything she could not to waste a second of it. If she set her sights on a challenge, she gave it her all, regardless of the end result.

It was the beginning of spring, when purely by accident she met Theodore Sterling. Just another wannabe river rafter, she thought. Watching him unload his gear, she became curious about his intent. His equipment was not like the stuff most of the regular visitors used, nor was it like the stuff used by the local guides.

This particular April, Riggins had been experiencing unusually warm temperatures, and they'd had a record snowpack that winter. *Mirabichi,* the Indian God of water, was about to turn loose his hydro power to flush the canyon of any winter debris. Anyone without the highest level of white water expertise, who dared to challenge his power raging through the canyons, might well find themselves on the last ride of their lives.

"Excuse me," Maggie said, halfway chuckling, "The side with the big hole in it has to go on top!"

"Thanks Miss. I wasn't sure. The directions for this plastic canoe blew out the window when I stopped for gas. This is the river to New Orleans, isn't it? My names Ted... Ted Sterling. And you would be?"

"Maggie... Maggie Rawlins. I just have to ask you. Have you ever done this before? This river is going to be running pretty strong for the next few weeks. Most of the rafting guides have even shut down their operations until they can get a better read on the conditions."

Maggie, as always, was the first to step forward if she felt that a stranger to the canyon may be underestimating the power of the rivers. This lone adventurer, not only looking very young, seemed to be mocking her, she felt, for her comments about the unusual water conditions.

The young man paused and smiled. "Well, miss– I assume it is miss– yes, I have done this before, but only a few times. Now let's see if I can remember...hmm. There was the river down south, I believe they call it the Amazon, but I think my most memorable ride was the one I took on that trickle they call the Zambezi through the Batoka Gorge."

Maggie had met other young fools and braggarts whose ultimate fate had led them to an eternal resting spot under a huge submerged boulder, never to be found again. But this guy was different somehow. There was something else about this one, and she just couldn't put her finger on it.

"Now, that was a trip! I lost a Kodak Brownie over Victoria Falls, as I remember. Boy, was that guy who loaned it to me pissed. Not another camera store for miles, and he was on the last day of his vacation. When the naked villagers 300 miles downstream found it a few weeks later in the belly of a catfish, they opened the camera and exposed all of his vacation film. Yes, I remember that trip well.

"I guess I'm supposed to sit inside this kayak contraption, here in this big hole. Most of my other trips I just hang my stuff around my neck, find a good log to straddle, and pray to God to keep me safe. What's your strategy, if you don't mind my asking?"

"Mr. Sterling, it seems that you don't take this very seriously so I won't waste anymore of your time." She turned to walk away. "You might want to put a note inside your vehicle before you hit the river, though. It'll make the authorities' job much easier when they have to contact your next of kin– just in case you don't come back, that is."

"Hey, hold on there, Miss Rawlins. I was just joking with you. How about we start over? By the way, this isn't just a coincidence that we're meeting. I've done a lot of asking around about a guide. Your name just kept coming up, and I was told that I might find you down here at the landing. I didn't mean in any way to offend you."

Maggie smiled. She had suspected that the young man had been kidding, but for her, the river was nothing to kid about. To raft, let alone kayak, in these conditions, should be left only to the experts, and even then it was extremely dangerous.

"If you will forgive me, Miss Rawlins, I would like to buy you lunch and get your feel of what I might be up against with this river of yours. I've been told that you know every inch of it and that there is no better person to ask. I need to know how I can make it from here down into Hells Canyon in one piece. How about it Miss Rawlins? Would you please accept my apology?"

"I will on one condition. From now on just call me Maggie."

"Done deal, Maggie, and you can call me Ted."

Having made his amends, Ted and Maggie strolled off to a nearby cafe for a light lunch while they discussed his proposed trip downriver.

Maggie turned and asked Ted, "Do you hunt?"

"Hunt what, Maggie?"

"Wild animals silly, things like that."

"No. The only wild thing I've ever wanted to slay was the wildness of the rivers."

Maggie pleased with his response, flashed him a broad smile. "I knew there was something we had in common."

With the current rate of melt off the mountain snowpack, he had to agree with Maggie that the erratic water conditions warranted a trip downriver by car before any attempts at the rapids could take place.

With his adventure temporarily postponed, Ted took the opportunity to learn more about Maggie's experiences and realized he wanted to learn more of the specifics of what made her tick. There was something special about this girl, but he couldn't quite put his finger on it. He had set aside two weeks to spend in the area during his summer vacation from his studies at the University of Montana in Missoula. He couldn't imagine a prettier girl in which to spend the time with.

Ted was in his junior year at the university, working toward his bachelor's degree in forest and wildlife management, and Maggie was all ears to learn about the subject. By the end of the afternoon, exploration of the river had become the last thing on either of the young couple's minds.

When Ted learned that Maggie had graduated from high school far ahead of her class and that she also had a great love of nature, he had an idea. If she hadn't already been offered or previously pursued a scholarship to college, he might be in a position to help her.

One thing he had not told Maggie was that his grandfather, as well as his father, had graduated from the University of Montana. He also failed to mention that his grandfather, when he had died, had bequeathed more than ten thousand forested acres to the university for research. In addition to that, his father was currently working as a research fellow at the university.

Maggie and Ted arranged to meet the next morning. They'd drive a route north along the river and possibly discuss Maggie's future plans.

That evening when Dan arrived home, Maggie ran out the door to meet him. "Daddy, oh daddy, I met the nicest college boy in town today. His name is Theodore and he is in college and everything…."

"Whoa there, little filly. Just what do you mean you met a nice *college boy* in town? Young lady, a boy who is attending college isn't called a *boy,* he is called a *young man.* Just what were you and this *young man* up to? Did you tell him you're seventeen years old? Did you tell this *young man* that your daddy is an avid hunter and rarely misses what he aims at?"

"Oh, daddy, don't be silly. It isn't like that. He's just a real nice boy. He just came to town to run the river and we started talking. He goes to college in Missoula. We were just talking about school, and he said he might be able to help me get a scholarship if I was interested."

"Did he happen to mention what he might want from you in return for this so-called scholarship?"

"Daddy, it wasn't like that. I told him all about you and mama and about what kind of work you did guiding and about how you love the outdoors just like he does. He is really nice, daddy. I would love for you and mama to meet him. I'm supposed to meet him tomorrow to drive the river, if that's okay. You can come with me if you want. Oh please, Daddy, say yes!"

"I think that's one fine idea. Hanna, dear, have you seen that .45 colt of mine? Maggie wants me to go meet her new college boyfriend in the morning, and I recently got the sights fixed on that old pistol. You just never know what kind of predator might be lurking down by the river. I sure wouldn't want any of us to get lured into a situation we're not sure of, unarmed. Now you go and help your mama with dinner, sweetie. We'll talk about this more after I get cleaned up."

As Dan headed for the hot spring, towel draped over his shoulder, Hanna and Maggie giggled like two school girls about to go on their first date.

"Maggie, I told you your daddy would say yes. You just have to learn that daddies watch over their young, especially their daughters, like a cougar with his harem. If you want to pet their cubs, you approach them with a great deal of caution, let them see that you mean them no harm. Then a mama cougar might even let you pet them. Now, daddy cougars, on the other hand, they like to size up another male, maybe even bat him around a bit with their big paws, just to show him he's the leader. If this young man is as nice as you say he is, your daddy will know. If your daddy doesn't knock that boy into the river with one of his big paws, I think he'll be safe. Now set the table, and then you can go pick out what you want to wear tomorrow."

Chapter 16

With heartfelt emotion, Dan described in his journal the day Hanna, Maggie, and he had driven to Missoula to deliver their daughter and her belongings to the university.

It had seemed like their lives had been swept up into the vortex of a giant tornado. Where had the time gone? What had begun as a quiet day, long ago at a diner in White Bird, the day he had fallen in love with Hanna, was now entering a new phase, and this was oh so bittersweet.

Standing silently, he gazed into Maggie's eyes. Expecting to see his little girl, he realized that his little girl was forever gone. Those eyes returning his love were that of an incredibly beautiful young woman.

They had agreed with Maggie's decision to attend the university, a decision that they knew would be best for her. But he also felt that life was now taking them on a roller coaster ride, transporting them on a journey through a mysterious portal in time to a place where he was to surrender his daughter into the hands of some unknown entity. He knew in his heart that when he and Hanna turned to walk out the door that day, they would feel as the eagles felt when their chicks took flight for the first time. Though she would always be their daughter and the love of both of their lives, she would from now on be driven by God's will.

As with all God's creatures, it was time for the parents to say farewell to their child. It was now Maggie's turn to spread her wings and take flight as her ancestors had done before her, her turn to explore the wonders of the world that awaited. Maggie had become a woman.

As they drove into the mountains and entered LoLo Pass, Dan reached out to Hanna and drew her closer to his side. He had seen the sparkle of pride in Hanna's eyes as she had witnessed her daughter's aura of beauty and confidence bloom. Yes, tears had been shed that afternoon, but they had been tears of love, not sorrow.

"Hanna, what say we stop over and spend the night in White Bird? We can get a room at one of those fancy motels, and if you're game, we could even brush up on our old baby makin' skills, if you have a mind to."

"Well, cowboy, if that old body of yours can manage to stay in the saddle on this young filly, maybe we'll just see if you still have any of that young colt spirit left inside you!"

Taking his eyes off the road just long enough to flash her a wide smile and snatch a kiss, Dan knew in an instant that everything was going to be okay from that day forward.

"You never know, Hannah. If you behave yourself, the new owners of the White Bird Diner might even let you–"

"Daniel Rawlins, don't say another word! If this filly hears one word out of your mouth about cooking or anything else food related right now, she just might come down with a hitch in her giddyup and have to spend the night in a corral by herself."

That day would be one that Dan would cherish for the rest of his life. The smiles and laughter they shared would remain in his heart and soul forever and would be the strength he needed to endure his pain and loss when his dear Hanna passed from this world.

Maggie, as she had always done, excelled in every class she took at the university. Ted, who had graduated with honors, as expected, was now living in Seattle where he had been given a junior executive job with one of his father's lumber companies.

The two of them had talked about marriage, but Hanna had managed to convince Maggie that with time apart, and with her still in school and Ted living in Seattle, it might be best to use their separation to temper the steel of the love they both had expressed for one another.

"Love," Hanna told Maggie, "is not just a feeling, but the heartbeat between two people." God has given us all a miraculous gift. That gift of true love when discovered, can never be eroded by time nor distance. And only you will know when it is true love, Maggie. You will feel the warmth of its presence in your soul."

Dan could still hear Maggie's words after she had learned of her mother's death. "Daddy, I can still feel mama inside my heart. I remember what she told me about what love is. Even now I can feel her love reaching out to me. I can feel her in my heart right now. She is telling me she loves me and that everything is going to be okay."

Dan had written in his journal that he would always treasure spending time alone with Maggie and exchanging some of their family's memories. Those times had helped to fill the void that Hanna's passing had created.

Two years had passed since Hanna's death when Dan received a letter from Maggie announcing her engagement to Theodore

Sterling. *Theodore.* Who in their right mind would name a child Theodore? Dan snickered. Well, according to the letter from Maggie, it wouldn't be long before Dan would find out.

The wedding was to be held in a church near Lake Washington, and the reception was to be a staged event at a private estate bordering the lake, with Mount Shuksan as its backdrop.

Once again, Dan smiled as he studied the invitation he had saved and read the details of the announcement.

> **"A reception to follow at the William Sterling Estate where the guests will be treated to the grandeur of Mount Shuksan. All attending are asked to RSVP."**

Even though Dan suspected he might not fit in real well with the upper crust that would be partying at the "William Sterling Estate," he had looked forward to meeting Theodore's family.

The wedding was to be held the following month, and Dan was going to be giving Maggie away at the ceremony. The only suit Dan owned was his bathing suit so he figured he'd better take a trip into Boise and buy some city folk clothes.

It would be a 650 mile drive from Riggins to Seattle, and with the pain Dan had been feeling in his lower back, an alternative means to get there had to be found. After making a few calls to some of his special friends, a military helicopter in need of maintenance just happened to be scheduled to fly to Seattle the following week.

Clearing his schedule, Dan arranged for his neighbor, David, to take care of his animals and watch over his place in his absence. Even though he would be getting to Seattle a few weeks early, he was excited about having the extra time to rekindle his relationship with Maggie before the wedding.

Nobody even noticed when the Huey lifted off from the ranger station at White Bird, and even fewer took note of its arrival at a National Guard Armory in Seattle.

"Just let us know when you're ready to go home, Captain Rawlins!" the pilot yelled as Dan walked from the tarmac. "We always like to help out one of our own!"

Dan smiled as he remembered what the pilot had called him: Captain Rawlins. Those boys running the show back home just couldn't ever tell anybody the truth, he thought. They couldn't have just told the pilot they had some guy needing to deadhead with them to Seattle. It had to be a "Special flight for a captain from the Department of Defense."

With what little time Maggie and Dan had alone together before the wedding, one afternoon they managed to take a cruise on Mr. Sterling's sixty-foot yacht on Lake Washington. Although they were not alone onboard– considering the boat came equipped with a captain as well as two stewards and a cook—the staff's presence was, for the most part, inconspicuous.

The crew had been trained well. They made themselves disappear like ghosts in the presence of any guests, only to appear, without being summoned, out of the shadows from time to time to refresh a drink or to replenish partially consumed silver platters of gourmet finger foods for their spoiled passengers.

Dan and Maggie took a few strolls together around the estate over the following days, watching in amazement as the grounds seemed to magically transform. The stage had been set and the chairs were all in place. With the expenditure of God only knows how much money, Ted's father had graciously stepped up and offered to foot the bill for the entire wedding. This was a godsend, because on Dan's budget, Ted and Maggie's only other option was to exchange their vows at a justice of the peace and hold their reception at the Riggins Café.

Dan found Ted's parents and extended family to be very hospitable and charming. Even though he sensed from time to time some underpinnings of wealth snobbery, overall, his visit with his future son-in-law's family went quite well.

He especially remembered one special moment during the ceremony he had not mentioned to Maggie. When the minister asked, "Who gives this woman to be married to this man?"

Dan paused, and then managed a faint, "I Do."

"Who gives this woman?"

Hell he thought, *I'm not giving Maggie to anyone. Loan her and a portion of her heart to Theodore maybe, but I'm not about to give him all of her.* As her father, he would retain the rights to a portion of Maggie's heart and soul that would remain with Dan and Hanna forever.

Not wanting to embarrass his daughter on her very special day, Dan morphed his character into one that any upper crust snob would have been proud of, and the wedding went off without a hitch.

The next morning Ted and Maggie departed on Mr. Sterling's private jet for a two-week honeymoon in Barbados, where the family kept a winter home. In the meantime, Dan took a taxi back to the National Guard Armory to arrange passage on the next transport heading east.

It was at the armory that day that Dan learned that Bill Sands had suddenly resigned as the chief deputy in Riggins and that his friend Dennis Boyd was promoted from his deputy position to replace him.

Eight months would pass before Dan summoned the courage to make his final entry into his journal.

Two months after the wedding, Dan received an emergency call from Deputy Willoughby, a reserve deputy from Riggins. Dan and Willoughby had been acquainted only on a professional basis at the time. Willoughby hadn't known about the close relationship Dan had had with his Maggie, so Willoughby delivered the news in a more professional manner than it would have had it come from Dan's close friend, Dennis Boyd.

"Mr. Rawlins, I just received a call from the police in Washington State," Willoughby said. "The Sterling family is trying to reach you. Your daughter Maggie and her husband Theodore left on a flight from Seattle yesterday en route to Missoula. They filed a flight plan with an approximate arrival in Missoula at 1600 hours, but they failed to arrive at their destination. As of now, no one has been able to contact them, and they are considered missing.

"Has your daughter contacted you, or do you know of any change of plans they might have discussed with you? Are you aware of any problems the couple may be having with the Sterling family that may explain why they didn't arrive in Missoula? Do you know of any reason why they are not returning calls to Mr. Sterling's family?"

Dan's heart sank and the blood rushing through his veins suddenly felt like ice water.

"Willoughby, get a hold of Boyd *now* and tell him I'll meet him at the office. Hell, no, there isn't any reason that I know of why they can't be contacted or why in the hell they haven't sho up in Missoula. I haven't spoken or heard from Maggie in two months. I have no idea why in the hell they were even going to fly to Montana." Immediately, Dan's mind shifted gears into a leadership role as he began barking orders to Willoughby.

"Get on the radio and alert the FAA and Civil Air Patrol that they might have a plane down. Notify Forestry to contact anyone they may have up in their lookout towers to be on high alert for anything unusual–smoke, a signal fire, anything at all. I'll make some calls when I get to the office. I know some people. Maybe I can get some choppers in the air in a hurry and start a search party."

When Ted's father learned of the events unfolding, the situation changed dramatically. With a Washington state congressman and a U.S. senator now inquiring about the missing couple, the combined search and rescue forces of Washington, Oregon, Idaho, Montana, as well as Wyoming, were all set into motion.

While everyone remained on high alert, scouring their radar screens and scanning their radio channels, trying to locate an emergency beacon from a possible downed aircraft, just miles to the west of Riggins, the single-engine Cessna 172 slowly sank into the frigid depths of a remote Hells Canyon lake.

Although Ted had originally filed a flight plan from Seattle to Missoula, routing his plane over the northern part of Idaho, Maggie had asked him to divert their course further south over Hells Canyon. Although it had been a clear day, Ted hadn't seen the flight of Canadian geese until it had been too late.

As the small craft disappeared from sight, Maggie, who had been ejected from the craft on impact, now lay floating motionless [illegible] surface.

[illegible] limp body was about to join her husband's, a shad[illegible]ppeared from the tree line and plucked Maggie

Sterling's unconscious body from the frigid water just as she was taking her last gasping breath. Placing her lifeless body on a bed of fern's he stripped her tattered wet clothing from her trembling body and gently tucked a bearskin around her to give her warmth. As the figure was placing a poultice on the laceration on her thigh where moments before the white bone of her femur glistened in the sunlight, Maggie regained consciousness just long enough to see the blurred image of an old man's face looking down at her.

For the next ten days the skies over the northwest were abuzz with low-flying aircraft, filled with personnel frantically searching for this influential man's son and his wife. With the news of a wealthy timber baron and major benefactor to education as well as those with political aspirations behind the search, no stone was left unturned, nor was any expense spared to rescue this downed pilot.

In all the media reports and pleas to the public to be on the lookout for the plane or its pilot, Maggie Sterling's name was never mentioned, only that Mr. Theodore Sterling was the missing pilot and that his wife was also on board.

After an exhaustive search over the millions of acres of wilderness encompassing the region, news reports concerning the crash began to fade. Nothing more could be done. No wreckage had been found, and the likelihood of anyone surviving had long since passed. It was now time to accept the couple's fate and terminate any further search efforts.

Ted's family held a memorial service in Seattle, but Dan had not been invited, nor would he have attended if the offer had been extended. Behind the cabin where he and Hanna had lovingly raised his beautiful Maggie, Dan placed a small white cross next to another one. The first had originally stood high on the hillside above the creek where they had lost their baby so many years before.

Almost a month had passed as Dan sat at his desk late one evening, pondering what he would do with the journal he had lovingly written for Maggie and had saved for her until she was grown. Now she was gone and would never know the secrets the journal held. What he thought would have been important for his daughter to learn about her life one day no longer mattered. None of it mattered.

"Dan, are you there?" the sheriff's radio barked. "Dan, come in. It's Dennis!"

"Go ahead, Dennis. I'm here. This is Dan, over."

"They found her, Dan! They found her. She's alive! Dan, did you hear me? Maggie is alive!"

"Where is she? Oh my God! When… where…? Where in God's name did they find her?" Dan sat there trembling, hearing words he never thought he would hear.

"She's in an ambulance on her way to the hospital in White Bird. She's alive but God only knows why. It's a miracle, truly a miracle. Get to my office as quick as you can, boy! We'll take my squad car; it will be faster, I'll give you the details of what they told me on the way. Just drive careful. Don't you go and kill yourself on the way into town." Twenty minutes later, on their way to the hospital in White Bird, Dennis filled Dan in.

"Two hikers found her, Dan. Can you believe it? They said that they were about a quarter mile off the road on a trail, just south of Lucile. They'd stopped in Lucile for lunch and just happened to take a stroll south along the river. They found a trail going up the hillside and saw some deer standing on the ridgeline.

"This guy's girlfriend wanted to get a little closer to take a picture, and then, hell, Dan, what's important is that they found

Maggie! You can ask them yourself. They're going to meet us at the hospital. Can you believe it? If it hadn't been for a few dumbass deer standing out in the open like that in the middle of the afternoon...."

Dan burst through the emergency entrance and headed straight for the double doors toward the patient treatment area. At the last second an ER nurse who would have been flattened had she not cleared the swinging doors before Dan got to them, stopped him. "Wait, sir. You can't go back there."

"My daughter Maggie is back there. You have my daughter. She was the girl from the plane crash."

Deputy Boyd quickly intervened. "Please excuse him, nurse. This is Mr. Rawlins. He's the girl's father."

"Your daughter is going to be fine, Mr. Rawlins. The doctors are with her, and she has been moved upstairs to the ICU. She is stable, but very weak. The doctor has ordered x-rays. It appears that she may have some broken bones.

"The best thing you can do for her now is to stay calm and let the doctors do their job. She needs to be cleaned up and hydrated. Your daughter has been through a major ordeal and is very lucky to be alive. Take a seat in the waiting area and I'll come and get you just as soon as the doctor says you can see her."

Regaining his composure, Dan did as he was told. Surveying his surroundings, he spotted a young couple dressed in hiking clothes and the female had a camera hanging around her neck. They were standing in the middle of the lobby area talking to a gathering of police officers, and a few men in dark suits. In his excitement he had walked right past them. He sprang to his feet and approached the couple, Dennis following behind.

"Excuse me, are you the people who found–" he began.

Cutting him off before he could finish his question, one of the dark suited men quickly moved between the couple and Dan. "Just one moment sir. What is your business here?"

Recognizing the posture of a government "yes man," Dan's blood began to boil. He had already been angered by the fact that Maggie had only been mentioned as an unnamed passenger in the missing plane. She seemed to have been insignificant to any of these people– up until now.

This man's authoritative, arrogant attitude had nothing to do with Maggie's well-being. Rather than being passive as he had been with the nurse, Dan quickly let him have it with both barrels.

"Look, you son of a bitch, if that is the couple that found my daughter Maggie, I want to talk to them, and I want to talk to them right now! If you don't want me to plant my unimportant foot deep inside your government ass, I suggest you get the hell out of my way!"

The color of Dan's face had changed from red to a deep crimson, and the veins in his neck looked like they were about to burst. Coupled with the fact that he was being escorted by a uniformed sheriff's deputy, the man in the suit decided to acquiesce. He stepped aside, moving slowly to relocate himself behind the others to a position of safety.

"My name is Daniel Rawlins," Dan announced putting his temper in check. "I believe that these two young people may have helped find my daughter Maggie, and I would like to thank them and ask them a few questions."

After receiving a nod of affirmation from one of the officers Dan moved forward, reached out his hand to the young couple, and in a soft, emotional tone, thanked the two strangers for saving

Maggie's life. Accepting Dan's thanks they introduced themselves as Travis Brown and Serena Adams.

Deputy Boyd and Dan bookended the couple and quickly, without opposition from anyone, whisked them toward a room, across from the lobby area where they would be able to talk in private.

Taking charge as if the other officials milling about had absolutely no reason or authority for even being there, Dan turned back to the nurse and barked out orders. "Nurse, we'll be in here if you get any updates on my daughter. I want to be notified immediately as soon as I can see her, and tell her doctor that I would like to see him as soon as he has her stabilized."

Over the next hour, Dan listened intently as the young man, Travis, retraced the couple's steps that day. They had been taking a drive north along the river when they decided to stop for lunch. His girlfriend Serena, a photography student, wanted to check out the wildflowers along the river behind the restaurant she had seen through the window.

They had walked about a quarter mile south of the town of Lucile when they saw four or five deer grazing on a ridge west of the highway. Spotting a trail leading from the edge of the roadway into the tree line, they thought they might be able to get a little closer to the deer without being seen. As they came around the backside of a large rock outcropping, they saw a large eagle looking directly at them.

At first, because it remained still on the rock without flying off, they thought that it might be injured. But when they reached out toward the bird, it made a loud screech, then effortlessly turned and flew a few yards up the hill, landing in a small meadow. Following so that Serena could take the eagle's picture while it stood with the rays of the sun filtering through the pines behind him, they suddenly heard the cries of a girl back in the trees.

When Travis went to investigate, he found a girl just off the trail in the shadows atop what appeared to be a bearskin. His first thought was that someone had maybe attacked her, or worse.

Serena stayed with the barely conscious girl, while Travis ran back to Lucile and called the police.

"When I led the officer back to the meadow, the policeman said, "Oh, my God. I think that might be the girl from the plane crash!" When he asked the girl if her name was Maggie Sterling, she raised her head and nodded yes. Then she fainted."

"I helped the policeman carry her back down to the highway, we laid her in the backseat of his cruiser, and the officer called for an ambulance. That is all we know. The police just got our names and told us to drive up here to the hospital in case the doctors had any more questions. Mr. Rawlins, we just arrived here a short time before you did. You and Sheriff Boyd are the first people we've told about how we found your daughter.

"Sir, someone had to have put your daughter there. She didn't have any shoes on, and she was very weak. That mountainside is really steep above where we found her. She couldn't even stand, let alone hike down from the top of that mountain. We didn't see or hear anyone else, but there's no way in the world she could have gotten there by herself."

"You said when you found her she was lying on a bearskin?" Dan asked. "Do you still have it? Did you bring it down with you?"

"No, sir. The policeman and I were just concerned about getting your daughter down the hillside and getting her some medical attention. I guess nobody ever thought at the time to bring that down. As far as I know it's still up on the hill. None of the other officers have said anything about it."

"Son, can you take me back up there and show me where the trail is?"

"Yes, sir, I'm sure I can find it again. It's not real easy to spot if you're driving, but I'm sure I can find it if I walk back down there."

"Well, son, you'll never know how thankful I am for what you did. You and Serena were very brave. You stayed with my daughter, not knowing anything about the situation or who might have been up there with you two. You saved my little girl's life.

"The police are going to want to get a statement from you about what happened. If you would, please temporarily forget what you told me about the bearskin. I'm also with law enforcement, and I'm a tracker as well. If you could meet me in Lucile later this afternoon, I sure would appreciate it.

"Right now I have to wait and see how Maggie is doing, but I do want to go back up to where you found her before any of these other people go traipsing all over the hillside and destroy any clues. Will you do that for me and just keep this between us for now?"

"Are you really a cop, Mr. Rawlins?" Travis asked, looking worried.

"Yes, son, I am," he said. To reassure the young man, Dan opened the badge case he kept in his pocket that held his Idaho County Deputy's badge.

"He certainly is, David," Dennis chimed in, reaffirming Dan's credentials. He had been quietly listening to the conversation while at the same time guarding the door.

"You can reach me at this number, Mr. Rawlins," Travis said, clearly relieved. "I have to take Serena home after we talk to the police, but we both live just a few miles from here.

If you don't want me to say anything, I won't– unless they ask about it, you understand. Serena and I don't want to get into any trouble."

"Dan, I'll tell you what," Dennis interjected. "Let me drive back down to Lucile with David here, and keep him and the location under wraps until you can meet us there. That way David and Serena can quietly slip out of here without being bombarded with a lot of useless questions. I'm going to go find the cop that brought Maggie here and talk to him as well.

"As it stands right now, Travis and Serena are just a couple of nice young people who came across an injured girl and did the right thing. They called the police, and that's where their involvement ends. We have their information, and if someone needs to follow up later they can, but right now let's just let a sleeping dog lie. You go take care of Maggie, and Travis and I will take a little ride back down to Lucile."

Chapter 17

As Dan walked into the room in ICU, tears of love welled up in his eyes. There lay Maggie who against all odds had survived it all. The agony and suffering she must have had to endure was incomprehensible to him. For twenty-two days this young girl had clutched onto life. Even the evil Seven Devils of Hells Canyon could not strip away her courage. She had faced down the fury of the giants of the canyon, and, unlike many others, she had survived.

Standing at her bedside, Dan gently stroked her hair, then kissed his sleeping princess on her sunburned forehead. How could she have possibly found the will to never give up? The mountains where her broken body had lain were filled with the predators of which nightmares are cast, yet she somehow managed to find an inner strength to hold them at bay. Holding her hand, somewhat leathered by so many days in the sun, he still hadn't fully absorbed what the doctors were trying to tell him.

"Mr. Rawlins, there is no logical reason your daughter Maggie should still be alive," Dr. Latham told him. "X-rays show that she had suffered a compound fracture of her left femur. We removed some debris from around the area where the bone had originally protruded through the skin and had begun to heal. Either your daughter set that broken bone herself or a miracle happened, but whoever or whatever did, applied a mixture of native moss and lichen as a poultice to help stop any infection. Mr. Rawlins, that type of poultice hasn't been used by the Indians–or anyone else, for that matter– in these parts for well over a hundred years.

"No matter what kind of scenario I have tried to conjure up, there is simply no plausible explanation of how your daughter, acting alone, could have set that fracture. Her chest x-ray shows a stress fracture to her sternum, which was most likely either caused when she was ejected from the plane or from the initial impact. That, combined with the fracture lines on the third, fourth, and fifth ribs, should have certainly immobilized her or caused her to go into fatal shock. There is simply no way that Maggie could have possibly moved about in that terrain under those types of wilderness conditions, let alone gather the nourishment that would have been required to sustain her life for that length of time.

"On top of all of that, when she was admitted the ambulance attendant said that she wasn't wearing shoes, and I confirmed that with the officer who found her. Mr. Rawlins, her feet showed no signs of trauma, none whatsoever. I myself have been up in those mountains countless times before, and you're a hunter and tracker. Can you explain to me how she managed to walk away from a plane crash in Hells Canyon without suffering even a small abrasion on the soles of her feet?

"I have been practicing medicine for over thirty years in this area. Either someone gave aid to your daughter, or this is one spectacular display of Godly intervention that someone needs to tell the pope about. Her survival is simply a miracle.

"Now, the next question is, who was it that helped your daughter, and where are they now? She wasn't molested in any way. Her injuries are all consistent with those possibly caused from some type of accident, and her superficial abrasions to her hands and face are no more than a camper might sustain on a weekend campout. Mr. Rawlins, I was told you work in law enforcement. Can you explain any of this to me?"

"No, Doctor Latham, I can't. Maybe when Maggie has had a chance to rest and feels like telling us, we'll both find the answers to these mysteries, but I don't have a clue. Right now all I want to do is say thank you to God or anyone else who protected her and brought my little girl back to me."

An acute trauma nurse entered the room. "My name is Molly Stevens, Mr. Rawlins."

Dan froze. He recognized the voice. As he turned slowly toward the woman, she recognized him. Molly Stevens had been the nurse at Hanna's bedside the day she had died.

Moving forward, she hugged him. "Mr. Rawlins, I'm going to take very good care of your daughter Maggie. You don't have to worry about a thing. "Your daughter has been through quite an ordeal. The doctors have put her into a medically induced coma, which will enable us to stabilize her blood count and glucose levels. For some unknown reason, she doesn't appear to be suffering from severe dehydration, but we are closely monitoring her vitals until Doctor Latham gets her blood work back from the lab.

"She will most likely be sleeping for the next few days if you need to contact family members and update them. The nursing staff has been instructed to remain with her for the next 48 hours so we can monitor any unusual changes in her condition. Someone will be by her side at all times. She has been alone long enough.

She must have had an angel on her shoulder." Molly shook her head. "She truly must have had someone from up above watching over her."

There was little more that Dan could do while the medical staff tended to Maggie, but there was time for him to retrace the events of the day and to try to get some answers before nature erased any possible clues from where she had been found.

He headed south to the town of Lucile where he met up with Dennis Boyd. Boyd had already arrived at the location with Travis, the young man who had found Maggie, and had assigned one of his reserve deputies to stand by at the entrance of the site to prevent any curiosity seekers from possibly contaminating the area. In a small town like Lucile you couldn't even open your window without the entire population of 152 curious souls knowing about it. So by now everyone in Lucile knew that their little town had just been put on the map.

As Dennis and Dan reached the meadow where Maggie had lain, the two separated, both scouring the area looking for any signs of how Maggie had managed to end up there. While Boyd checked the surrounding tree line, Dan made his way to the large ponderosa where he found the bed of ferns that Travis and Serena had described.

Then he saw it. Piled in a heap, he spied the bearskin that had covered Maggie's body. Boyd joined Dan, and with the sun about to fade, they made the decision to secure the area for the night and return the following morning. Cordoning off the area would ensure that nothing would be missed, or accidentally disturbed, which would ruin any chance at all of solving this mystery.

Dan took the skin in his arms, and the two of them headed back down the hill. Riggins was just eight miles south. They decided that

Boyd's office would be a better place to headquarter and examine the few facts they gathered, away from any curiosity seekers or members of the press who would undoubtedly be descending on Lucile like vultures once the word got out–which in all likelihood, already had.

Back at the office and spreading the bearskin out on a table, Dan was suddenly struck by something strange. "Dennis, look at this. Look at the fat in these creases. This bear is a fresh kill, or at least it hasn't been exposed to the sun for any length of time. Feel how supple it is. This wasn't some old bearskin someone just picked up; this came from somewhere up in the canyon within the last few weeks. I think we need to get Burt Summers over here to take a look at this. I've hunted a few of these over the years, but he's processed hundreds of bearskins and knows a hell of a lot more about what I'm looking at than I do.

"Take a look at this. Look at these slash marks up near the neck area. Nobody shot this bear. It looks like its neck was ripped open. What do you think, Burt?"

"Well, you two, I can tell you this for sure. You're right about one thing. This bear was killed by something other than a gun or a bow and arrow. There's not a penetration mark anywhere on this skin other than the neck area. Another thing, look at these tears in the hide. I have seen those before. You're not going to believe this, but in my opinion, an eagle or more than one eagle killed this animal. I would say this bear was a young sow, maybe 250 to 300 pounds. From these tear marks, she was hit by something very sharp several times, and probably bled to death. Who or whatever did this sure as hell knew where her arteries were, because by the looks of where they tore through her throat, they sure weren't amateurs at killing.

Getting ready to leave, Burt turned back to Dan. "You should be able to backtrack on this. As fresh as that skin is, you shouldn't have any problems finding some of her scat or where she's been feeding. With the dry weather we've been having, a big girl like that has left plenty of evidence to follow, and the rest of her has to be scattered somewhere. All that shouldn't be hard for a tracker like you to find. Good night, gentlemen, and good luck!"

Although Dan wanted to head out the next morning, Dennis convinced him that it would be best if he stayed behind with Maggie. "Dan, you know as well as I do that I can come up with a dozen good men ready to help out. All you have to do is say the word. Hell, she was up there for twenty-two days. If we get on a trail, we could be up in those canyons for days before we find anything. You need to stay close to town. Maggie needs you here."

Reluctantly, Dan agreed. If there was something to be found, the men Dennis spoke of were just as experienced at tracking as he was, and they certainly knew Hells Canyon as well as he did.

Leaving the follow-up on the bear mystery to Dennis, Dan went to his cabin, got a few changes of clothes packed, and headed back to White Bird. Maggie might wake up at any time and be able to provide the vital information he needed to explain what had happened to her and her husband–the information that so many of those involved desperately sought.

Four days later, a knock sounded on Maggie's hospital room door. "Afternoon, Daniel. How is our girl doing?"

Dan had been sitting at Maggie's bedside, gently massaging a medicated lotion into the recovering skin on her palms.

Nurse Stevens, who was sitting at a small desk in the corner of the room, charting Maggie's daily progress, looked over her wire-rimmed glasses and grimaced as she saw Dennis's boots, "Excuse me, sir. If you weren't aware of it, this is a hospital, not a horse stable. If I'm not mistaken, is that horse dung all over your boots?"

"Begging your pardon, miss. I was in such a hurry, I forgot my manners. I assure you it won't happen again."

"No, you don't understand. It's not even going to happen now. There's a janitor's closet two doors down the hall on your right. Please take yourself and those filthy boots out of this room right now and don't come back unless you can walk into this room on clean bare feet.

You can also go ahead and dispose of what I can only imagine is a disgustingly filthy pair of socks inside those boots while you're at it, and grab a pair of booties from the nurse's station."

"Yes, ma'am. I'll be right back. Dan, by the way, we found something I think you need to hear about. It was just about a quarter of a mile–"

"Sir, I said out of here, now. What part of now do you not understand?" Nurse Stevens had clearly had quite enough.

"I'll be right back, Dan."

Fifteen minutes later, with his hair combed and his cowboy hat in hand, Boyd attempted his second entry into the room. Extending his hand, holding a small bouquet of flowers toward the nurse, Dennis did a shallow bow and extended his offering of peace. "These are for you ma'am. I'm sorry about my crudeness earlier. Can you ever forgive me?"

Abruptly closing the cover on the paperwork she had been working on, Nurse Stevens snatched the floral offering from Boyd's outstretched hand and stomped around him toward the door. "If you or Maggie need me for anything," she told Dan, "I'll be in the nurses break room. I think I need to go wash my hands!"

Boyd stood there, bewildered for a moment, but quickly recovered. "Well, Dan, old boy, you're not going to believe what we found."

For the next two hours, Dennis reported that he, along with three other men, had gathered at the clearing where Maggie had been found. They found a few deer tracks alongside the footprints that Dan and he had left the day before, but nothing appeared to have been disturbed in the overnight hours before their search had begun.

They also found some elk tracks that had entered the perimeter of the meadow from the west. These tracks indicated that the elk had been walking "heavy," according to the depth of his tracks on the relatively dry soil. It had either been one hefty elk, or something had been weighing him down.

For the next two days they followed the tracks into Hells Canyon to the top of a ridgeline where the tracks suddenly disappeared. The men divided up and searched for several more hours in concentric circles from the last sighting, but they found nothing. Not a single track.

"The strangest thing about the whole thing is that from the time we left the meadow and headed up the canyon, the four of us were being followed by a flock of eagles. I'm serious as hell, Dan. It wasn't the whole group the entire time, but at least one circled either directly above us or just off to our side at all times. When we bedded down at sunset, several would land in the treetops around our perimeter, and it was like we were under surveillance. They just watched us, as if to anticipate our next move. I have to admit it gave me the willies."

Boyd went on to explain, "We followed the elk tracks to where they ended back in the trees. There we found this large, matted, grassy area encircled with rocks, and it looked like someone or something had been sleeping there. There wasn't any fire pit, no evidence of human waste, no remnants of a campsite whatsoever–with one exception. Yellow meat bees swarmed all around us, as if they were looking for another meal.

"Jim Higgins found two spots on the rocks about fifty yards from that area. Someone obviously had been drying some salmon or trout because Higgins saw splotches of residue fish oil on one of the slabs of granite, as well as remnants from dried salmon flesh down in the cracks of the rocks and fish bones scattered on the ground.

"Do you know how far it is from that spot to any place in these canyons where someone could catch a salmon? We figured, at a minimum, ten miles. It would have taken a man with a pack mule two days to haul an ice chest up those hillsides to where we were. Number one, they would have had to keep the fish fresh, and number two, where in the hell would they get the ice? They would have had to climb up into the peaks, and they sure as hell didn't do that. With the exception of the crags in the shadows of the high peaks, all the snow is gone. And would anyone haul a whole fish instead of a fillet? What were the bones, including the skulls, still doing up that high? None of this makes any sense, Dan, and I mean none of it.

"Even if someone had come across the plane crash and found Maggie, why not a signal fire? Hell, you know as well as I do that the skies around this place were filled with planes looking for anything, anything at all. Why wouldn't someone, if there was a someone, try to signal? It just doesn't make any sense."

"Dennis, you are a dear friend," Dan said when Dennis finished. "I don't have any answers either and maybe we never will. The doctor told me this morning that they've stopped sedating Maggie, and that maybe this evening or sometime tomorrow she'll be cognizant enough to answer a few questions. As soon as I know anything I'll call you. Now go find your boots and get the hell home. You've been a godsend, but it's time you head home and get some rest. Tell the boys how much I appreciate everything they've done, and that I promise I'll make it up to them."

"You don't owe any of us a thing," Boyd objected. "You would have done the same for any one of us–in spades. I'm going to get out of here and leave you two alone, but call me the minute Maggie comes around. No matter what time it is, call me."

It didn't take long before a hospital staffer, who had overheard conversations about Maggie's story, saw an opportunity by breaking the news. No one in the media had yet reported on her rescue, and the chance to possibly make a few bucks, get their name on TV and become famous, if only for a few minutes, was simply more than this person could resist.

"Channel 4 news desk, can I help you?" The floodgates opened and the story about a woman surviving twenty-two days in the wilderness hit the wires, and the media buzzards took flight.

Who was she? Where was she? What was her name? Did anyone have any pictures of her or the scene? Are there any bloody photos?

Deluged with telephone calls, the hospital public relations office had finally had enough, and after several hours released the following information:

"We are not at liberty to release the woman's name or any extensive details.

We can tell you that two days ago, a lone female we believe to be a survivor from the plane reported missing on a flight from Seattle, Washington, to Missoula, Montana, was rescued and admitted to the White Bird, Idaho, regional hospital. Her condition is critical but stable, and authorities are continuing their ongoing investigation."

Well, that was all it took. Mr. and Mrs. William Sterling knew exactly who the lone female was–their daughter-in-law, Maggie Sterling. The search for their son that had been halted only a few weeks before, now resumed with vigor. Washington State politicians, anxious for an opportunity to once again seek out any camera lens they could find, joined in the foray. This was an election year in Washington State. The Maggie Sterling story provided a priceless opportunity for free media exposure, for a few of the not-so-popular windbags to blow their own horns, and it all had been dropped squarely in their laps.

Dan, who had gone to a motel to shower and change, turned toward the television as a reporter from a Lewiston, Idaho, station appeared on the screen. Looking like he could hardly contain himself, he smoothed his tie and craned his neck, posturing himself toward the camera as if he were a national TV news anchorman instead of the fill-in weatherman. He began:

> "This is Jerry Wilson, KXTN News Channel 4 with breaking news. We have just learned from CBS News in Seattle that a female survivor from the missing plane that authorities have been searching for over Idaho, Maggie Sterling, has been found!"

Dan froze. Not only was this idiot spewing a line of bullshit a mile long, he was supposedly quoting additional information received from a "credible unidentified inside source," at the hospital. About the only thing that was true in the story so far, was her name and the state where authorities had found her. They had no clue what injuries she sustained.

The only way they could have obtained her name was from someone within the hospital itself or through the Sterling family in Seattle.

For this very reason, when Maggie had first been admitted to the hospital, she had been brought in as a Jane Doe, with very few other details being provided. Dan had seen to it that the Sterling family had been notified the first day they had found Maggie but not Ted, he didn't think this "breaking news" would have come from them. Further he had cautioned Ted's father about going public too soon regarding Maggie. He had made it very clear to Bill Sterling that if the story broke in the news, every dumbass who could get a hold of a horse or a pair of hiking boots would be tromping all over Hells Canyon in search of their son's aircraft wreckage.

If that were to happen, any tracks that Maggie may have left behind that could lead searchers to the plane and their son could be easily obliterated. He advised Sterling that until they could learn more information from Maggie, it was imperative that details about the location where she had been found be held in strictest confidence. Sterling had agreed. So far, the name of the town of Lucile hadn't been mentioned, but Dan knew it was only a matter of time before it was.

He hoped that Maggie would soon regain consciousness and be able to fill in some of the blanks. Dennis and the other trackers had come to a dead end. Without more clues from Maggie as to the events that had unfolded, the crash site and the cause may never be known, nor would the body of Theodore Sterling ever be recovered.

Dan had to get Maggie out of that hospital, and it had to be done immediately before the media swarmed the place. Once again, Dan's experience and background in keeping things quiet told him he had to formulate a plan.

After making a quick call to his old friend Rick Mears and requesting him to handle the logistics of the operation, Dan made his way back to the hospital to speak to Doctor Latham and Nurse Stevens.

Deputy Boyd had put out an announcement that a press conference for the media would be held in front of the White Bird hospital at 4:00 p.m. At that time updates on the investigation would be announced.

Dr. Latham had agreed that Maggie had improved to the point where she could leave the hospital, but on one condition. She must continue to be monitored by a nurse. Nurse Stevens immediately volunteered for the job.

Shortly before 4 o'clock, while most of the hospital staff took up positions at windows to watch the media frenzy out front, an unmarked ventilated box van backed up to the loading dock at the rear of the hospital. As everyone focused on the media circus, Nurse Stevens, accompanied by Dan dressed in a hospital orderly's uniform, rolled what appeared to be a deceased patient covered with a sheet down the hallway toward the hospital morgue.

Making a quick detour at the hospital service elevator to the basement, they made their escape out a side door, completely unnoticed. Boyd, dressed in a delivery man's coveralls, lifted the rear door of the truck, loaded his passengers, and as unobtrusively as he had arrived, pulled away and headed south toward Riggins.

By the time 5 o'clock rolled around and still no officials came out to address the media, speculation of what had happened spread over the crowded courtyard like mule piss on a flat rock. The media was furious. They demanded that the hospital allow at least one of their numbers to act as a mediator for the news pool, and to allow that individual to confirm Maggie's presence.

Pressured by hospital administration who desperately wanted to avoid any negative publicity at all cost, Dr. Latham acquiesced and led a female reporter to room number 305 on the third floor. Swinging the door open, he announced, "There she is. Ask her anything you want."

Seeing only an empty space that once had obviously been occupied by a bed, the woman yanked off her mask in disgust. The media outside had been hoodwinked. Fuming, the woman turned toward the elevators and loudly blurted, "You, Doctor, Latham and this hospital are going to pay for this, I can assure you. My audience is going to demand some answers!"

"Good day to you, miss. Tell all your fans that Doctor Latham wishes them well!"

While the reporters were battling with the hospital's administration for more information, Dennis made a sweeping turn around a chain barrier at the entrance to the road that led to Dan's cabin. Dan had posted a sign that read, "Danger! Road Closed. KEEP OUT!" USFS (United States Forest Service). They were now just a short distance away from the peace, serenity, and total privacy that Maggie so desperately needed for her recovery.

They had one more thing left to do: debunk the media's original source and spread confusion. They needed to divert any possible lookieloos away from the area where Maggie had actually been found. Radio and television stations were being inundated with telephone calls from people, wanting to remain anonymous but who just happened to know the exact spot where the girl had been found. Some of them who wanted their fifteen minutes of fame even claimed that they had been present at the location when Maggie was found.

By the time Rick Mears's "Operation Deception" was completed, callers had claimed to have found Maggie in over fifteen different locations around the northern half of the state, ranging from the Bitterroot Range down to the peaks of the Sawtooth Mountains. There had even been one claim that she had been found in a cabin near Orofino, and another that said she had been found sitting on a riverbank, fishing near Moscow and was suffering from amnesia. By the time they were done, this girl seemed to have been found everywhere, except on the hillside south of Lucile.

By the next morning, the media finally got the hint, and the story faded from the headlines. What was once a story that was going to get some cub reporter the Pulitzer Prize, had now turned into an occasional news bleep stating that government agencies were still investigating and had no comment regarding the condition of the survivor.

Maggie's rescue quickly became back-page news, just as Dan had wanted.

National news outlets were choosing not to expose their front line reporters to possible ridicule on national television, so on advice of their legal departments, they simply looked the other way. Their experience told them that someone in the government, for whatever reasons, was firing blanks over the heads of those small-town news directors just to lead them on a purposeful wild goose chase, and they weren't about to take the bait. When and if the real facts were ever released, then they would step up to take credit for the story.

Chapter 18

With an impromptu hospital room set up in the bedroom of the cabin, Dan gathered up a bedroll and headed for the stable. There just wasn't enough room in the cabin for him, Maggie, and Nurse Stevens, so Dan decided that rather than accepting Boyd's offer to stay at the Sheriff's Office in town, he would rather stay close and bunk with his mule Molly. He wanted to be readily available to help with Maggie's needs, but also provide security in the event any reporters had managed to figure out where she was hiding.

"Molly, old girl, you're going to have to move over, cause you're getting yourself a new roommate. At least for a while," he mumbled as he entered the stable.

While Molly had been okay with sharing her stall with Dan, she wasn't real thrilled with the second freeloader that followed. Annie the beagle was not about to have her relationship with Dan outshined by any old mule. But as cuddly as she might have been snuggling next to Dan, she brought with her some atrocious snoring issues, of which Molly was not overly pleased.

Just before 6 o'clock, Dan heard a voice. "Mr. Rawlins? Wake up, Mr. Rawlins."

Dan leaped to his feet. "Is something wrong? Is something wrong with Maggie?"

"No, she's resting peacefully now," Nurse Stevens reported, "but she is becoming more responsive. She woke up about an hour ago and asked who I was. She also managed to stand up and walk with me to the restroom. She went back to sleep, but I'm hopeful.

I think that very soon, Maggie is going to be back with us. I just wanted to let you know.

"I'll come and get you when she wakes up again. She still doesn't know where she is or what's happened. She asked for Ted first thing and wanted to know where he was. We need to go very slowly at first. She's going to have a lot of emotional issues to deal with. I just wanted you to keep that in mind before you see her."

A little past noon, Nurse Stevens summoned Dan, "Mr. Rawlins, Maggie would like to see you now."

As he entered the cabin, he found Maggie standing before him. Nurse Stevens had managed to utilize some of the items she had found in the cabin that had most likely belonged to Hanna.

Maggie's auburn hair that had been matted by her many days in bed, now lay in gentle waves to her shoulders and framed her beautiful face. Nurse Stevens had lovingly brushed her hair and applied some of Hanna's makeup to Maggie's face, restoring her radiant glow, and, she had dressed her in a pink, ankle-length nightgown for her reintroduction to the world.

When Maggie saw her father for the first time her eyes filled with tears. "Daddy, daddy, I was so scared. I couldn't do anything for him. We were falling, and there was blood everywhere. I couldn't help him, daddy. Then we hit the water."

Blotting her tears, Dan took her into his arms and whispered, "It's going to be okay honey. There was nothing you could have done. You're alive, Maggie, I was so afraid that I had lost you, too."

Nurse Stevens remained for two more days, and then decided that Dan could now oversee Maggie's further recovery. She made her way back to White Bird in Sheriff Boyd's personal vehicle so as not to arouse any suspicion on her return to town. But before she left, Nurse Stevens gave something important to Dan, an eagle's tail feather.

"Here, Mr. Rawlins, Maggie might want to keep this. When she arrived at the hospital and we undressed her, we found this feather tucked inside her clothing. Maggie probably picked it up somewhere when she was out there in the wilderness and found some kind of comfort in it. She probably doesn't even remember it, but maybe someday she will want to have it."

Over the next week, Dan and Maggie talked about the events that had led up to the plane crash. Ted and she had taken off early that morning for a trip to Missoula. He had just recently obtained his private pilot's license and had been anxious to use it. He wanted to fly over a large timber stand his family owned in Northern Montana.

With logging operations underway, Ted felt that was as good a reason as any to try out his new license. He wanted to do some flyovers to make sure that the timber removal was on schedule and that the operation wasn't having any negative ecological effects on the surrounding areas.

Ted had told Maggie that they had just crossed into Idaho and that Hells Canyon lie just south of where they were. She had asked if it would be okay if they could change course and fly over the peaks where her mother was buried. The detour would only take about an hour longer, and Ted, without hesitation, said yes.

They had made one pass over She Devil Peak, heading south, when Ted turned the plane to circle one more time so Maggie could take a picture. The sun suddenly blinded them for just a second. Unknowingly, Ted had turned the plane directly into the path of a large flock of birds heading straight for the windshield.

She heard a loud bang and the plane shook violently. Wind started rushing into the cockpit. When she looked over at Ted, his face was covered in blood, the windshield had a huge hole in it, and there were feathers flying everywhere.

The engine all of a sudden made a loud banging sound, and then the plane started going down. She tried to help Ted and kept calling his name. She remembered looking up to see the water, and then everything went black.

She didn't know how long she remained unconscious, but she remembered seeing the face of an old man. He looked like an old Indian. He was stroking her forehead and trying to put something in her mouth. Sometime later, she didn't know how many days it had been, she woke up to see the man moving around her. She remembered that she was wrapped in a type of fur blanket, and when it was getting dark he would stack rocks around her. She didn't understand what he was doing, but the rocks were really warm. Every time she woke up he would be there, trying to get her to drink water from his cupped hands or feeding her dried pieces of fish. But he never spoke.

She thought the whole time she had been dreaming. The last time she saw the old man, he was walking away next to a big elk into the shadows of the trees. The next thing she knew, she awoke, and she was in the cabin.

"Daddy, I know Ted is dead. I knew it before we crashed. There wasn't anything I could do. But there's one other thing I remember. I remember the eyes of the old man who helped me. I didn't feel scared. I thought I knew him because I had seen his eyes before. I just couldn't remember where."

Maggie's recollection of the events began to explain how she could survive for twenty-two days in that wilderness. But who was the man who had taken care of her and gotten her to the meadow where she had been found?

She remembered his eyes? He was an old man that looked like an Indian? Dan's blood began to run cold.

"My God, Maggie try. Try hard now. Do you remember anything else about the man? Do you remember him ever holding you? Was he holding you the first time you saw his eyes?"

"I don't remember, but I'm sure that I recognized his eyes. It was like maybe when I was little. Like his eyes have always been in my dreams."

Well, Maggie didn't remember, but Dan sure as hell did. He remembered the night of the accident, the night someone had wrapped an infant in a sleeping bag and saved her life. It couldn't be the same Indian who had handed him that little baby that morning up on the hillside the day of the accident could it?

From that day on, whenever Maggie would mention her memories of the man's eyes, Dan would tell her that it was probably just a coincidence, that the man just resembled one of the old Indians she had seen before. Perhaps he looked like one of the old men up at the Nez Perce reservation she had seen before when he and Hanna had taken her to watch them dance at their festivals when she was little. He told her that it was simply a fond memory of a happier time she was drawing upon to ease her fears after the plane crash and nothing more.

Two days later, Dennis Boyd pulled up in front of the cabin, accompanied by Ted's father, William. After a brief greeting and a hug from her father-in-law, Maggie politely excused herself by saying that she needed to get some air and was going for a walk. Although she had been in love with his son, Maggie had always felt that Ted's family had never really accepted her.

Even on the days that led up to their wedding, while she'd stayed at their estate in Washington, Ted's mother seemed to go out of her way to show up with some local Seattle debutant that Ted either knew or had dated in high school or prep school before he had met her.

"Oh, Ted, look who's here to see you! You remember Paula." Or, "Look, Theodore, Avery, or Melissa, just couldn't wait to tell you how wonderful it is to have you home."

Yes, Mrs. Sterling had gone to extraordinary lengths to draw Ted's attention to every beautiful socialite girl she could find, right up to the time he had said "I do" to Maggie. Now Maggie had little or no interest in rekindling her relationship with her father-in-law.

Of all the things Dan had discussed with Maggie over the last few days, the fact that Maggie's name was never mentioned in the news reports concerning the missing plane was not one of them. Dan didn't think Maggie needed to learn the details of that, so he had purposely left them out of their conversations.

Although Maggie had never slighted Ted's family, Dan's intuition told him that the relationship between Maggie and the Sterling's was, for whatever reason, definitely strained. He felt it best to just mind his own business and not press the issue with Maggie. He would give Ted's father what information he knew about the search for his son while Maggie was out getting some fresh air.

He spent about two hours explaining in detail how six of his friends, all very experienced trackers, had searched for over a week, attempting to backtrack from where they had found Maggie.

He repeated what Maggie had told him about what had occurred before the crash, and based upon her last recollections, they were fairly confident the plane had gone down somewhere up around the peaks in Hells Canyon.

The fact that the last thing Maggie remembered seeing before she blacked out was water, it could only be assumed that the small plane had impacted the surface of one of the many high-mountain lakes in the area and had sunk.

After reviewing government typographical maps of the area, they pinpointed several lakes that may have been the impact site, however, no oil or fuel floating on the surface had been seen, no pieces of wreckage, personal belongings, nothing!

Without sending divers down to the bottom of every lake in the area it was almost impossible to identify the wreck site or retrieve either the plane or their son Ted's body. Further, with winter about to arrive in the high country, it wouldn't be long before the lakes began to ice over. To send divers to search now would be simply too dangerous. A search like that would have to wait until the following spring.

Mr. Sterling thanked Dan for everything he had done. He may be a man living on a palatial estate, but his roots back in the forests of Montana informed his understanding of the situation. Before he left, he handed Dan an envelope and said that inside were some funds he had put together for Maggie to help her out until Ted's personal affairs had been settled. If the worst had happened, the life insurance Ted had purchased on himself for Maggie wouldn't be available until a death certificate could be issued. Therefore, if

Ted remained missing, it could be as long as seven years before he could legally be declared dead.

Pausing at the door, Mr. Sterling turned to Dan and shook his hand for the last time. "You tell Maggie I always thought she was the perfect wife for Ted. Tell her she is always welcome at our home and that I only wish the best for her. If she needs anything at all, tell her she can always contact me."

When Maggie returned and opened the envelope, inside she found a cashier's check in the amount of five million dollars, payable to Mrs. Maggie Sterling, with a notation stating it was payment in full for death benefits.

Without asking any questions, Maggie folded the check, placed it back into the envelope, and said, "Thank you, Daddy." She never mentioned Ted's family again.

Three more weeks passed, and the snow was again making its way down from the north. Maggie's body had almost fully recovered, but her heart had yet to heal from the loss of Ted.

Maggie had become Hanna's daughter. Though not of Hanna's blood, Maggie had been raised by a woman whose character had been molded by the ancient spirits of the Nez Perce. While Dan had been away hunting, Hanna had been home, building Maggie's strong independence.

The morning finally arrived when Maggie told Dan she was leaving. Heartbroken, but masking his emotions, he knew deep inside he had to let her go. After all, she was Hanna's creation, and he knew a wandering spirit could not be caged.

Maggie had made plans to rent an apartment near the university in Missoula so she could be close to some of her friends while she began trying to mend the torn fabric of her life. She had been offered a job at the university, but she had declined.

Being financially secure, she could now do what she wanted. She became a volunteer at one of the orphanages, as well as tutoring children at an Indian school.

Chapter 19

As Dan sat at his desk for the last time that morning and entered the final words of his life into his journal for Maggie, he remembered a letter Hanna had written. He had found it by her bedside, addressed to Maggie, and had given it to their daughter after Hanna's death.

My Dearest daughter Maggie,

One day you will become a woman showered, not only by love, but by great sorrow. Many years ago, my people were driven from their lands, and many lost their lives defending those principles they thought were right. In life you must learn to compromise. You must learn to change the things you can but also learn to accept and live with the things you cannot.

Fight for what you believe in, Maggie, but learn to accept fate, and do not allow sorrow or defeat to overwhelm you. With death comes new life, and with life comes death. The two can never be separated nor can they ever be fully understood.

There once was a great Nez Perce chief, whose name was Joseph. In 1877, for five months he led my people in a fight against the government to drive the white man from our lands. Because his heart told him that there could be no compromise or compassion for anyone not of his tribe, many of his people had been killed.

In the end he watched the sorrow of a mother shed her last tear and her heart stop beating as she lay alongside her dead child. It is written that it was then that Chief Joseph stood on a hilltop much like those that surround you now and spoke to his people.

"Hear me, my chiefs. I am tired. My heart is sick and sad. From where the sun now stands, I will fight no more forever."

With time come the changes of the seasons, and with the changes of the seasons come new life and revitalized hope for a brighter future. Maggie, my sweet daughter, you are my brighter future.

Chief Joseph was a courageous warrior, but he had lost the will to compromise for a brighter future for his people. For that reason he lost the battle.

When life hands you difficult situations, if overwhelming sorrow should find its way into your heart, remember my words that I repeat once again to you:

With every life comes death, and with every death comes life. The two can never be separated.

When I lost your sister, I had thought it was the end of my life. Summoning the angels to act as His emissary on a cold winter's day, God reached down from the heavens and touched the three of us.

I always suspected that you knew you were not of my blood, but you chose not to challenge your heritage. I never questioned your love for me and your father.

The love you poured into my life could never have been greater. The love you gave to me was the love only a daughter could give– a daughter who had been created through your father Daniel's and my lifetime bond of marriage and love for you.

I will never know why God called your birth mother home that cold winter's night. The answer to that question is not ours to know. Why God chose to summon your sister from our lives and deliver you in return, will also remain one of those unanswered mysteries of life.

The unfettered love of your father tempered my faith, but it was God's will that delivered you into my arms, an orphaned, beautiful baby girl. With all your love and your wondrous spirit, you gave me back my life. You were the peace offering from God when I had questioned my faith. What had been God's plan when He had given your sister life? What words had He spoken to that old Indian that had made him cry?

Though God had challenged my faith that day at that roaring creek's edge, my faith in Him never wavered.

This is your life, Maggie. Live each day as if it were your last. Never stop giving from your heart to others as you gave to me. Hold strong your faith in God, and know that He will never forsake you. Finally, always know that no matter where life may take you, you are the reflection of your parents, and that someday we will all be together again for eternity. May the eagles carry you through life upon their wings.

I love you,

Mama

Chapter 20

As always, when Dan opened the back door, his faithful companion Annie took off like a shot toward the creek, bellowing like only a beagle on the hunt can.

"Damn it, Annie, shut up, girl. You're going to wake up everybody in the entire canyon!"

Oh well, he thought. Why not? This is a special day. "Go get 'em, Annie!"

Dan smiled. Just listen to that little ferocious bundle of joy that wouldn't hurt a fly bugle! Why shouldn't he get to hear her on the hunt, hear his loyal companion just one last time? He was sure that in the days to come, David and Kris would forgive him for allowing Annie to shatter the peace that early morning.

That morning, Dan fried up a pile of bacon and nearly a dozen eggs. He was going to be taking a hike later that morning, and even though Annie wouldn't be joining him, she sure did love fried bacon.

It was time. He placed a note on the desk for David, then retrieved the deerskin suit from the trunk at the end of the bed he had worn at his wedding, and packed it in his saddlebag.

Laying his guns out on the bed, he took one last look around, then closed the bedroom door.

"Come here, Annie. I know you're not going to like this, but I have to put your leash on. You can't come with me today, girl. You're going to go stay with David and Kris for a while." Heading out the door with Annie in tow, he turned for one last look at the place that held so many loving memories.

"Morning, Dan. How goes it this beautiful morning?" David asked.

"Fine, David, just fine. And yes, it is a beautiful morning. Today is my birthday, and I thought I would take a trip up to the peaks and visit Hanna."

"Well, it sure is a beautiful day for it. You going to take that loudmouth mutt of yours with you? She sure could make one hell of an echo up there in Hells, I bet."

"No, not this time. David, I need to ask you for a favor. I thought I might spend a few nights up in the peaks around He and She. Maybe even do a little fishing. I kind of want to just spend some quiet time walking around a bit by myself, without Annie and Molly bugging me while I'm there. If you wouldn't mind, would you check on Molly and maybe keep Annie inside while I'm gone? I've spotted a few lion tracks around here the last few days, and I wouldn't want them to get hurt."

"Sure, Dan, not a problem. Maybe I could take Annie for a ride to the vet and let him do a little fancy work on those vocal chords of hers." David chuckled at his own joke.

"If she starts bugging you, be my guest, my friend. By the way, I'm going in on the trailhead just east of where the tourists always park at Windy Gap. That's where I took Hanna to see the peaks on our first trip there. I'll leave the keys on top of the jeep's rear axle, just in case you need to use it while I'm gone. I left the cabin open if you need anything, and if Maggie happens to come by, I left something for her in the safe. The combination is written on the wall behind the refrigerator, if she can't remember it."

Stepping forward, Dan gave David a manly hug and patted him on the back. "Well, my friend, I guess that's about it. I wish Kris was up so I could have told her goodbye. You sure have been a great friend, David, you and Kris both."

As Dan was turning and heading for the jeep, David suddenly got a queasy feeling deep in his gut.

"Dan, hey Dan, are you okay? Is something bothering you? We can take a walk down by the creek if you want."

"No, today everything is going to be just wonderful. Take care of my babies for me, will you? I'll see you soon."

That was the last time David ever saw Dan Rawlins.

It was just about sunset when Dan reached the trail that headed up to the summit of She Peak. By the time he arrived, the pain he felt from the cancer within him was now almost unbearable.

Although he had wanted to summit She Peak on his birthday, he decided that he would spend the night with Hanna and make the final trek up to He Summit in the morning. His body simply could not go any farther that day.

As dawn broke the next morning, Dan stood, dressed in his wedding adornment, for the first time since their marriage and started up the trail. Today would be the day that he and Hanna would once again hold each other in their arms. At the top of the summit, Dan knelt for a time at Hanna's gravesite, and, in silent prayer, he summoned her spirit. God's angels answered with a forlorn chant.

From the valley, winds began to rise in spiraling thermals up to the heavens, and with them appeared a flock of soaring eagles. First a female, trailed by a young female fledgling, landed atop the rocks, little more than a few yards from where Dan now knelt.

"Hanna and Maggie, it's time for me to join you. I have missed both of you so much. I have so much to tell you about your sister, *Maggie*. You would be so very proud that she shares your name with you.

"Now I shall sit with you and see where we will fly together. At sunset, my angels, I will fly away with you. The three of us will soar together to the heavens to watch over our Maggie, wherever life takes her.

"I must leave you now, Hanna, but for just a brief time. I must go to where the spirits are calling my name. I must go to He Devil where I will soar into the skies above and once again caress you."

Just as the sun was about to set on the valley of Hells Canyon, Dan stripped off his mortal clothing and stood on the summit of He Devil. As he gazed upon She Devil Peak, he watched as a huge male eagle swooped down and landed on an altar of stone just above him.

Suddenly, in a swirling cloud of mist, the mighty eagle morphed in front of his eyes into the body of the old Indian, who had watched over his family in life.

Beckoning him forward with a wave of his hand, the Indian looked on as Dan paused to place a single eagle feather atop his deerskin tunic, then turn and step forward to the edge of the precipice. The old Indian suddenly disappeared up into the sky in a column of swirling dust, just as Dan stepped forward to join Hanna and baby Maggie in the heavens above Hells Canyon.

When Dan failed to return home after the third day, David contacted Dennis Boyd, and the two of them headed up to Hells Canyon to look for him. The jeep and the keys were exactly where Dan had told him they would be.

"I think we'd better take the jeep and go up to the peaks and look for him," David told Boyd. "It's not like Dan not to follow a plan. Maybe he's hurt. He's been complaining about pains in his back. Maybe he can't hike out on his own.

"I'll call dispatch and contact the forest service and let them know," Boyd said. "They might have some people up around here that can look for him as well."

Knowing Dan as well as they did, it didn't take them long to locate what remained of the clothing Dan had shed a few days before.

"Dennis, have you found anything around here. Tracks, or anything where Dan might have tried to walk out?"

"I found some prints at the top of the peak and what looks like his deerskin pants and shirt with an eagle feather tucked inside. But surely he wouldn't have left those behind. He has to be around here somewhere.

With their focus on the ground for any evidence of Dan's visit to the peak, neither of them ever looked up. If they had, they would have witnessed one of the most beautiful pirouettes performed by a family of three eagles atop the rising thermals of Hells Canyon.

For the next few days, Dennis had found so many men from the area who wanted to volunteer to search for Dan, you would have thought that someone had discovered gold in the hills of Hells Canyon. By the end of the third day the tracks from the searchers left a crisscrossed, web-like pattern atop the mountainsides that would have made any of God's arachnids proud. But nothing more than the initial find of Dan's clothing was ever found.

Returning from the search, David entered Dan's cabin to see if Dan had left any clues. On the top of his desk he found an envelope with the name David written on it. Inside David found what he considered to be an impromptu Will. He also found a letter addressed to Maggie.

Chapter 21

My dear friends, David &Kris:

If you are reading this, I want you to know that I am truly happy. I am now with Hanna and our baby Maggie in the Valley of the Angels. I have finally shed the physical pain I have been suffering for quite some time, and I am now free to wander the woods I love so much, at peace with my dearest love, Hanna.

It was not my wish to burden you with Molly and Annie, but there are few others that I would entrust their lives or their futures to. I have left my guns and a few other things in the bedroom for you, David. Think of me occasionally, and know my spirit will be there with you. In Molly's stable, you will find a hidden panel just below where I hang her harness. There is a duffle bag inside with a few things I would prefer that you destroy. There may be someone from the government asking around about certain things, and it would eliminate a lot of questions and answers if the contents I am speaking of simply no longer existed.

Feel free to remove any of my clothing you think you could use, David, as well as any of my personal things that you may have some use for. Kris, this goes for you as well regarding what I have left in the drawers and closets of Hanna's. When Maggie was here during her recuperation, she went through most of Hanna's things for anything she treasured, but what remains of Hanna's personal things, Maggie had no interest in keeping.

Like I told you, David, the combination to the safe is written on the wall behind the refrigerator. In it you will find an envelope with some cash that should cover any expenses for the animals, as well as any cost of upkeep on the cabin for the next four or five years, I suspect. I would have offered you the land and the cabin, but that will have to be Maggie's decision as to its disposition.

Inside the wrapped deerskin you will find a journal. I wrote it for Maggie to read one day to explain some things about her life that Hanna and I had never found the courage to tell her. It may be of some interest to you and Kris as well. I only ask that it be given to Maggie when she learns of my passing. What she does with it will be her decision.

I have written down the names and telephone numbers of some of Maggie's friends in Missoula, as well as the contact information for the Sterling family in Seattle should you have need to contact them.

The jeep and the radio equipment, as you know, belong to the county. However my pickup is all yours. You'll find that I signed the title over to you, and you'll find it is in the glove box. Molly's trailer and the other equipment around the place now belong to you.

The furnishings in the cabin I will ask you to leave for now. I don't feel as it would be right to give any of those things away at this time. Once again, that will be Maggie's decision, as I have told her in her letter.

Well, I guess that's about it my friend! Both of you have been wonderful neighbors, trusted friends, and Hanna and I considered you an extended part of our family. If you ever get up to Hell's, look up and give us a wave. We would love to have the chance to see you both again from time to time.

One last thing. I don't know if you knew it, David, but Annie prefers sleeping at the foot of the bed. She snores a bit sometimes, but she is really a great companion. You'll get used to it with time....

Well, you two, it's time to say see ya, but not goodbye.

I have a beautiful little Indian girl waiting for me to ask her to dance up in Hells Canyon, so now I must go.

May God shed all of His blessings upon both of you, and may you live a long, happy life together.

Wherever you two may go or whatever situation may embrace you, always know that you shall have guardian angels watching over you. With all my love and gratitude,

Your friend forever,

Daniel R. Rawlins

P.S. David, when you talk to Doctor Morgan, tell him I said he was right. That would not be the way I would have wanted to die, either. He'll know exactly what it means.

David contacted Maggie in Missoula that day. Just before midnight he saw a vehicle arrive and the lights go on inside Dan's cabin. Maggie answered the door and invited David and Kris inside. It would be a long night ahead for all of them.

David went over everything Dan had written in the letter and then gave a second letter to Maggie. Even though David and Kris had insisted that Maggie stay a few days with them, she politely thanked them but said no.

Having lost her mother Hanna, recently losing her husband Ted, and now her father, Maggie was not only having to deal with this loss but the combined grief of losing all of them.

David explained what her father had said about the journal in the safe, but Maggie had all the information she could possibly deal with already. She thanked them for all they had done and for accepting the responsibility for the animals, and told them she needed to have some time alone to absorb all that had happened.

Not long after dawn, David was awakened suddenly by Annie's barking.

The beagle had been alerted by the sound of a vehicle being started and driven away. That was one of the last times Kris and David ever saw Maggie in person.

When David went to check to make sure the cabin was secure, the front door had been left wide open, and the journal, once again wrapped in the deerskin, had been placed back inside the open safe. This time Maggie had placed three eagle feathers atop the bundle.

The day finally came when I had to bid farewell to David and Kris and head south to Boise to catch my plane back to Oklahoma. The time I spent there will be one I will always remember. The story written in Dan Rawlins's journal definitely gave me pause. Miracles happen every day all around us, and maybe I should take the opportunity each day to think about Dan and Hanna. Just a few seconds, a mere flash of time on mankind's eternal clock, look to the sky, and bow my head to the angels that I now truly believe do exist.

As I waved my goodbye and headed down the lane, I looked in the rear view mirror toward Dan's cabin and watched in amazement. Standing tall at his post, casting off the subtle tension caused by my visit to his hallowed ground, the eagle sounded a loud screech, launched his body into the air, and in a slow, gentle spiral, rose into the sky and disappeared from view.

It was then that I knew that this majestic bird was really an angel who had granted me brief access to the secrets of his realm.

Once a stranger who had so recently entered this mystical lair of privacy and secrecy uninvited, I was now departing, quietly thanking Dan, Hanna, and Maggie for allowing me to be a very special friend.

From Windy Gap where he had first danced for me, an angel had become my friend, giving me special access into the Rawlins family's lives. Was this the angel, Dan Rawlins? This I do not know.

In life each of us makes choices. I hope mine will be the one that will make him smile when I am called to look into his face. I, too, would so much like to be one of the lucky ones to be given that special gift someday,–that gift that will lift me high into the sky, to soar on warm thermals above God's masterpiece. Maybe I will have the opportunity one day to ask Dan Rawlins if he was the eagle atop his cabin.

What an honor it would be if I should be invited to soar as an eagle. Maybe, just maybe, I may be asked to dance with them as one of the Angels of Hells Canyon.

Epilogue

The following spring after Dan went away, Sheriff Rick Mears retired suddenly from the Idaho County Sheriff's Department and moved somewhere back east, some said to Alexandria, Virginia, where he was working for the government. But nobody really knew for sure.

Dennis Boyd had been offered the chance to run for Mears' office but for some reason he had declined. Even though everyone knew that Dennis Boyd would probably run unopposed for the sheriff's job, he had also decided, for no apparent reason, to pack up his bags as well. He quietly left Riggins, some say to work for a private security contractor based in Seattle, Washington.

Last year when I talked to David about writing a story about Dan and Hanna, he gave his blessings and suggested that I shouldn't show any restraint in telling the whole story of Dan's life in Riggins. Dan had not only been a wonderful, caring friend, he and his wife Hanna had been saviors in more ways than one. So now David felt that their whole story could be told without the fear of anyone's retributions, not even from threats of intimidation by the government.

With a tone of bitterness, David told me that shortly after Dan's death, their hidden sanctuary back in the forest had been visited more than once by unidentified men driving unmarked government vehicles. From the smudges that had been left behind around the locks on the Rawlins cabin doors, it was quite apparent to him that someone had, without invitation, made more than one entry into the structure.

It had not come as much of a surprise to David when he received a notice from the Department of the Interior, Bureau of Land Management in Washington D.C. notifying him that the land where the Rawlins cabin stood was part of the National Forest.

They wrote that the Rawlins cabin was to be removed by the Forestry Department within the next thirty days, and that his own cabin had also been illegally built on government property. David's notice stated that he was ordered to immediately remove all present structures, and that he was to vacate the property within thirty days or he would be subject to arrest.

Molly was given to the Forest Service where she now lives a pampered life carting park rangers around mostly in Hells Canyon, and Annie, now too far up in years to hunt, still rests at the foot of David and Kris's bed. Dan had only ever lied to David and Kris about one thing. They still haven't gotten used to that damn beagle's *snoring!*

Made in the USA
Lexington, KY
07 November 2016